Ember of War

Daniel Dickinson

Fedowar Press, LLC

www.FedowarPress.com

ISBN-13 (Digital): 978-1-956492-58-3
ISBN-13 (Paperback): 978-1-956492-59-0

Edited by Heather Ann Larson
Cover design by Getcovers
Interior Design by D.W. Hitz

EMBER
OF
WAR

DANIEL DICKINSON

Introduction

Centuries can pass in the blink of an eye, the one constant through anyone's life, is where they were when war started. For many, living peacefully in the countryside means upending stability to support the growing conflict. Through it all, it is not so much how war changes, but how the people react. There will be those manipulated into fighting, not in the name of some Kingdom's idealism, but for preservation of life. Others will pledge their loyalty to a crown that sees them as pawns to move about the board. Then there are the wild ones, so enamored with their lust for life, they throw it into the meat grinder. None of them matter though, not in the long run. The world will continue to turn. They will one day be forgotten. Even the reason the war started will be lost in the tapestry of history. Embers of war turn to flames that consume the old ways. Leaving behind ashes of what once was, what could have been, and will never be. It will make way for new life, new adventure. Destruction will force new heroes to rise and fight the oppressive forces lurking in the shadows of ash and smoldering embers.

The Kingdom of Xonthian

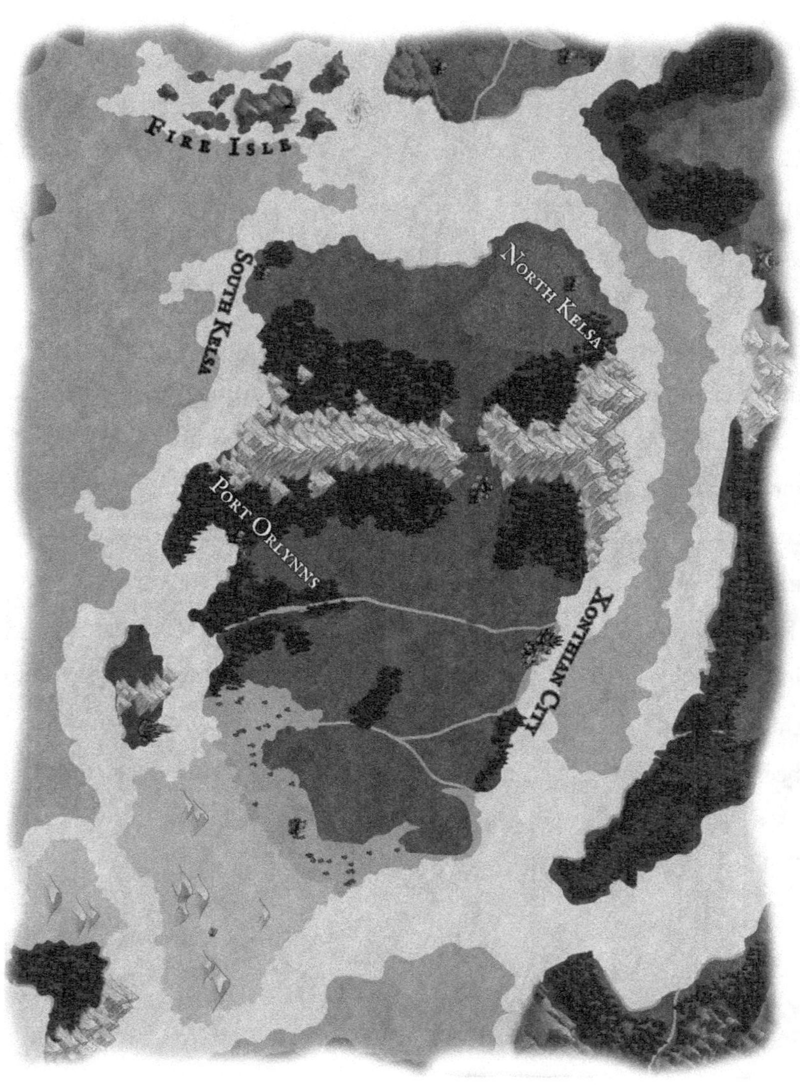

Ember
of
War

Chapter 1

CARNIVAL OF LIFE

MAGIC WAS A PART of his life. In fact, it was all he knew. Korrith breathed it and felt it caress his skin as he rode through the city. It was all around him. It enveloped his thin body like a heavy, warm blanket. His bright, grey eyes sparkled in the afternoon light as he prodded his horse toward the festival grounds on the eastern side of Xonthian City.

The city was made up of a patchwork of wood and stone buildings that stretched out along the beach. His slightly crooked nose flared as his lungs inhaled the salty air blowing in from the north.

"Korrith, over here!" Sorrna called, waving a hand in the air to catch his attention.

Korrith smiled broadly and waved a gloved hand at her. He slid down from his saddle and tied the reins to the hitching post nearby.

Sorrna ran over to him and gave him a big hug, causing him to grunt audibly in response. Sorrna's body was small in stature, but well-proportioned and slightly rounded. She wore blue-grey dress that swayed freely below her bosom down to her heels. A grey cotton shirt with soft folds covered the upper portion of her body.

"So good to see you," she said before kissing him softly on the lips.

He blushed slightly at the attention. "It's good to see you, too, Sorrna. Did you miss me?"

"Of course, silly!" she said as she wrapped a slender arm around his. Her blue eyes sparkled in the light. "Did you get them all enchanted?"

"You knew where I was?" he asked as they walked toward the main thoroughfare, where games of skill were being played.

"Of course, I did. I'm nosy, remember?" She grinned.

Korrith smiled, stopped, and took her mousy face in his hands and caressed her cheek. "You are that. But yes, all his majesty's cannons have been enchanted. It was a lot of work and took some time to complete. That kind of spell craft takes its toll," he said.

She glanced up and kissed him again. He lost his breath as his heart raced in his chest. He had missed her touch, her smell, and her smooth, warm skin.

"Well, we can relax now," Sorrna said as she placed her arm around his and continued down the row of sideshows and games.

Korrith watched as children and adults alike laughed, while attendants counted copper coins and yelled for passers-by to join them for a game of chance. Intermixed with these were stalls where farmers sold their latest harvest and craft goods. Bakers sold freshly made bread, while other stalls prepared hot meals for visitors. The air was filled with the smell of cooking meats and spices.

As they came to the end of the row, Sorrna stopped and giggled uncontrollably. "Look at that stuffed king. It looks so silly. I must have it!"

Korrith laughed and walked over to the booth where several other townsfolk were laughing and playing.

"I'd like to try," he said as he handed the man two copper pieces.

"Korrith?" A man beside him laughed. "Nice to see you outside of work!"

Korrith turned to see an acquaintance from his time at the king's naval yard. He couldn't recall the man's name.

The older man put an arm around Korrith's shoulder and ushered him away from the game booth. "All that iron enchantment takes its toll, doesn't it? Get them all done?"

Korrith laughed nervously. "Yeh, they're fixed."

"Good!" the man said, and spun back around, a smile on his face. "Well, we're finished here. You two have fun!"

Korrith nodded and waved his good-byes.

"Friend?" Sorrna asked.

"Co-worker, from the naval yard."

"You a magi?" the booth attendant asked as he looked Korrith over.

Korrith appeared like anyone else at the festival. He was wearing traveling breeches, a plain wool shirt, and gloves.

"What does that have to do with anything?" Sorrna asked, her voice rising to an accusatory pitch.

Korrith put his hand on her shoulder. "It's okay, I'm used to that question." *He must have heard my conversation with that co-worker,* Korrith thought.

The attendant pointed to a handwritten wooden sign which hung under a basket where the player would try and collect as many apples as possible. It read: "No Mages Allowed."

"If ya is a filthy magi, I suggest you find some other place to be," the man said, then spat at couples' feet.

Korrith took Sorrna's hand in his. She glared over her shoulder at the game hawker as she was led away. The man turned away in disgust.

"It has gotten worse," she said as they walked down the next row of stalls and games. Korrith nodded, and a frown replaced the grin on his face.

"Why do you put up with the *magi* slur?" she asked with a look of revulsion on her face.

"Because I don't need to exasperate the issue by getting into a fist-fight," Korrith said, a little more irritably than he intended. "I'm sorry, I didn't mean to snap."

Sorrna dropped her hand from his. "You should tell the king about it. People should treat mages equally."

"He knows," Korrith said.

"Then why doesn't he publicly embrace the mages and their abilities?"

Korrith shook his head. "I don't know. I don't work directly for the king. As far as I am concerned, I'm just hired help."

His abilities in the magical arts were deep. He could enchant fire and explosions, which led him to work for the shipwrights when they built some of his majesty's royal fleet. Sorrna knew that too.

"It's an outrage. Every day, every month, it gets worse for us. We get shunned and put in the corner," Sorrna said. "We're just as normal as anyone else around here."

Korrith took a deep breath, and the scents of the fair went unnoticed as he turned to comfort her. "Sorrna, as long as there are mages in the world who continue to advance the darker aspects of magic, like necromancy, the rest of us will be discriminated against."

"It shouldn't be that way. We haven't done anything wrong," she said, peering up at him.

"No, we haven't. Come on, let's go home," he said as he wrapped an arm around her shoulders and led her down the thoroughfare toward the city. "Let's find joy somewhere else."

Korrith ran a finger along Sorrna's shoulder, trailing it lightly down her arm. She shivered in response as goosebumps spread across her skin.

"Stop," she giggled as she pressed closer to his naked body.

"That's not what you said a few minutes ago," he said, inhaling her scent mixed with the musk of their lovemaking. It permeated the bedroom.

She raised herself on one elbow and peered into his eyes, then kissed him before she lay back down in the crook of his arm. "Behave, or I'll make you go another round."

"I need food first," he laughed.

Sorrna patted his sunken stomach. "You are wasting away."

He smiled and stretched like a cat lying on its back. Sorrna mumbled about being comfortable before rolling over with the blankets and exposing Korrith's bare body.

"Hey!" he said as he made a grab for them.

"Go, get food. Bring me a sandwich when you come back."

"Bring *me* a sandwich," he mocked as he sat on the edge of their bed to slip his breeches on. He stood and tied the drawstring. "Would her highness like something to drink?"

"Oh, yes, she would," Sorrna said.

Korrith walked to the kitchen, where the hearth smoldered dimly. He tossed several logs in, then whispered an incantation and snapped his fingers. The embers in the fireplace burst into flames, causing the newly placed logs to roar to life.

Their small house sat on the eastern side of Xonthian City. It was a modestly-furnished wooden structure with a stone floor and only one bedroom. There were no interior walls except around the small wash closet next to the bedroom.

Korrith shifted his attention to the table in the kitchen, where a loaf of bread sat on a wooden tray he had hand carved. It was ugly, uneven, and wobbled on the flat surface of the table. He pushed it with a finger to make it jiggle and smiled. He was not a very good carpenter.

He pulled the knife sitting nearby closer, along with the wheel of cheese from the opposite side of the table, and cut several healthy slices. He did the same with the bread and placed both on the tray. He repeated the process with a salami hanging near the fireplace. He replaced it when done and shifted his attention to the wash barrel sitting next to the window. He took out two goblets, washed them quickly, and glanced outside.

The sun turned the sky orange, as if it were ablaze. Streaks of clouds high in the heavens gave it the appearance of smoke, adding to the fiery overtone.

As he glanced back to his preparations, he caught the sight of Edrin coming down the road, toward the gate to their house. He sighed and set the goblets down on the table.

"I'll be right back," Korrith said as he walked to the door and opened it.

Sorrna peered up over her shoulder with a puzzled look, but didn't get a chance to ask anything. Korrith stepped outside and closed the door behind him.

"Edrin," Korrith said in greeting. "This is an unexpected visit."

Edrin stepped up to the small wooden porch leading into the house and smiled cordially. He was a small, stocky man with wide blue eyes. Short hazel hair framed his slightly rounded face.

"Sorry to call on you at this hour. I thought you'd like to know there's a merchant hiring up all the mages he can find."

"And that was important enough you had to come all the way out here?"

"Oh yes," Edrin replied. "The money pays double the king's wages. Plus, the work is guaranteed."

Korrith scratched his head in thought. Having a stable income would be nice, and at double the usual pay, he and Sorrna could finally afford to move out of the city and away from all the bigoted people.

"Come talk to him tomorrow night at the Stone Flame. That's where he's staying," Edrin said.

"Alright, I think I will," Korrith replied. "Thank you, Edrin."

The man smiled and nodded. "Of course. Sorry to interrupt you."

"Nonsense. Have a good night my friend," Korrith said, and held his hand out. Edrin took it and gave it a firm shake.

The short man wandered back the way he came, leaving Korrith standing in front of the wooden shack he called home. He glanced up at the sky one more time, and the illusion of it burning. A shiver ran down his back. He dismissed it and returned inside.

Chapter 2

INTRODUCTIONS

Korrith stood at the door of the Stone Flame. The building took up one of the four corners at the main square of the city, standing several stories high. Horses and carts clicked by rhythmically as he put a hand on the thick door. Music from inside seeped into his ears as if he was being charmed into entering. He took a deep breath, pushed the door open, and stepped inside.

The smell of stale beer, stew, and unwashed bodies assaulted him. The dim light of a fireplace, candles, and a hand-worked iron chandelier caused shadows to flicker in the corners of the large common room.

Men, women, merchants, and off-duty city guards talked and laughed in a cacophony of voices. They sat at the dark wood bar and at various tables scattered around the room. Flagons, mugs, plates, and tableware clattered like random punctuation to their conversations.

Korrith walked toward the bar before he noticed Edrin sitting at a table in the corner with several men he didn't recognize.

"I'm tired of being spat on," one of the men said as Korrith walked over.

"Greetings," Korrith said, causing everyone to snap their attention toward him in surprise.

"Oh, Korrith, it's you," Edrin laughed nervously. "You startled us."

"I apologize, I didn't mean to."

"Please, have a seat. Gentlemen, this is the other mage I mentioned would hopefully be joining us," Edrin said, clapping Korrith on the shoulder. "Glad you came, my friend."

"Of course. The prospect seemed too good to be real," Korrith said as he took the offered chair next to Edrin.

"I assure you, the offer is real," a voice said behind him.

The men looked to see a tall, handsome man with a narrow nose peering down at them. Raven black hair ran over his shoulders as if a waterfall of shadows flowed down his back. It was his eyes, however, that caused Korrith to involuntarily inhale. They were deep red, standing out against his pale features.

"Now that we are all here, please allow me to introduce myself. My name is Sengue Bebedor. I am in need of such talents as you have sitting here tonight." His raspy voice was barely audible over the din of the tavern.

Sengue took a seat across from Korrith and glanced around the table, a smile spreading across his thin lips. "I will pay you each twenty-five silver pieces a day for your services," he explained softly.

"Doing what?" Korrith said, somewhat harsher than he meant. He didn't trust something about Sengue.

The stranger smiled at the question but nodded as if agreeing with his apprehension. "I have a shipment coming into Port Orlynns. I need you to bring it here, to me."

"Isn't that what mercs are for?" Edrin asked, although Korrith could tell he didn't care. He knew his friend too well, and twenty-five silver a day was all his friend heard.

Sengue nodded. "In most cases, yes. However, this shipment needs a magic user's touch."

"What's the catch?" Korrith asked.

"No catch. You will travel to Port Orlynns, paid for of course, and then escort the shipment from there. All you have to do is renew the enchantment upon the cargo every day."

"What's the cargo?" one of the men asked.

Sengue sat back and waved a dismissive hand. "My team and I recently uncovered a sarcophagus belonging to a great general from the before times. I am bringing him home to Xonthian City for burial."

Everyone sat in silence, lost in their thoughts. Korrith wasn't sure; something in the back of his mind told him to stand and leave. But the promise of so much silver for a two-week journey from Port Orlynns to Xonthian City was hard to ignore.

Finally, Edrin stood and put his hand out. "You have yourself a mage," he said, shaking Sengue's hand in agreement.

Like a broken dam, the other two followed suit and shook the stranger's hand before congratulating one another on the easy pay.

"Come on, Korrith, join us. We'll make it a trip if the two of us are there. We can catch up on old times," Edrin said, slapping Korrith's shoulder as if he were trying to coax a stubborn mule forward.

"Yeah, alright," Korrith said, and held his hand out to the man in front of him.

Sengue smiled broadly before taking the offered hand, shaking it enthusiastically. "Good, good. Please ready yourselves and meet my driver outside of town in two days. He'll take you all south and pay you for the travel there. You'll receive the last payment when you return. Now, if you will excuse me."

Korrith nodded and watched as the stranger stood and wove through the crowded taproom before ascending the stairs to the rooms above. He shifted his attention back to Edrin, who was ordering a round of drinks. The two other men had departed after a quick but polite farewell.

"We'll be rich!" Edrin beamed as he sat back down and slapped a hand on the table.

Korrith folded his arms on the table in front of him and glanced at the smooth, beer-stained surface. "I don't know, Edrin. That guy doesn't feel right."

"Nonsense, you're just nervous to be away from your lady for that long," Edrin laughed.

Korrith snickered.

"Besides, you're the one always telling me you just need one large payday to get you out of here. This will be it."

"True. I... I just don't know. Maybe I'm just worried. That's a lot of magic being used in the open."

"Bah, those bigots are too dumb to realize it. You'll be safe at home by the time they find out."

Korrith looked up as the barmaid delivered two mugs of ale.

"This round is on me," Edrin said with a wide grin as he paid the woman.

Korrith took the offered mug. The hoppy smell of ale wafted through his nostrils, lifting his spirits.

"To our future," Edrin said as he raised his mug.

Korrith followed his friend's salute, their glasses striking together with a muted sound. The two friends drank deeply before setting them down with a thud.

"Ugh, if we're going to drink anymore tonight, we're getting something stronger," Korrith laughed. "You cheap bastard."

Edrin placed a hand on his chest at the accusation. "Me, a bastard?"

The two laughed uproariously. It melded with those around them, their spirits high at the prospect of the future.

Chapter 3

<hr>

ZEAL

THE SUN BURNED THROUGH the flimsy curtains of their house. The light penetrated his eyes, causing them to throb with pain. Last night's revelry threatened to vacate his stomach through the way it entered his body. He wanted to curl up and die.

Sorrna had other plans, however, and crawled up the length of his nearly naked body to straddle his lower back. His face pressed into the pillow, and he groaned in protest.

"Come on, you drunkard. Get up. I made you something to eat and drink to help with your hangover," she cooed in his ear, sending goose-flesh down his back.

"Do you have no pity for the dying?" he asked.

"Nope."

He moaned and threw the pillow over his head as he tried to force the nausea down.

She giggled, slid off his back, then straightened her muslin shirt. It fell around her thighs as she walked toward the table near the hearth.

Korrith rolled over slowly and took a deep breath as the world righted itself. He braced himself on the edge of the bed as he sat up, where he waited for the room to cease its spinning.

"Good, you're moving," Sorrna said happily. She poured some dense, black liquid into a mug and set it next to the plate of bread and eggs.

"Shh," Korrith said as he stood, waving a hand at her feebly. "Not so loud."

A chuckle escaped her lips as she sat down.

Korrith took his seat at the table and took a sip from the mug. The bitter, dark flavor assaulted his senses. Surprisingly, it eased the tension in his head and stomach. He ate quietly as she watched with bright eyes, studying him as he moved purposefully through the meal.

"You're too good to me," he said, wiping his lips with a napkin. "I love you. You know that, right?"

"I do. It's a good thing, because I spoil you enough," she said with a smile.

He returned her smile with his own.

"So, are you going to tell me how it went last night? What this job is?"

Korrith described the stranger to her, leaving out none of the odd feelings the man gave him. She asked probing questions about the job itself, including whose sarcophagus it was. He didn't have an answer and told her what the man had said, paraphrasing only slightly.

"I don't know, Korrith. We need the money, sure, but it also sounds dangerous," Sorrna said as she cleared the dirty dishes from in front of him.

Korrith took a drink from his mug and set it down again before continuing. "I don't think the job itself is dangerous. Sengue, on the other hand? He gives me the creeps. I can't explain it," he said.

Sorrna set the clean plate down in the rack and sat down at the table. "If you feel this is off, then don't go. We'll be fine. We always are."

"I'm sure it's nothing. No, I'm going to go. We need the money. We need to get out of this city," Korrith said as he stood. He walked over to his shirt and put it on, followed by his boots. "I need to go get some travel supplies before we go."

He gathered his coin purse and attached it to his belt, which he put on around his slender waist. He walked over to Sorrna and placed a warm, passionate kiss on her lips.

"I won't be long," he said against her mouth.

She pushed him away and flapped a hand in front of her face as if dissipating the stench of eggs and the black drink.

He laughed and kissed her nose before he spun around and left the small house.

"Magic and magi—they are a type of sin. Sin as deadly as magic has driven our world into ruin. Magics are the Gods' and the Goddess's language. When mortal men use it, it is the most loathsome, defaming, unclean thing in the universe. Magic, a hypnotic melody at first, has become embraced by men of power. And as with any sin, undermining man's nature reverses the harmony of his power, dismantling him of his nobility, woefully deranged, erratic, in interminable leagues of darkness. So shall magic cast men's souls into the abyss."

"Magic is a violation of the Gods' and Goddess's laws, rebellion against their authority. Sin, and by proxy magic, looks like a cloud no larger than a man's hand yet holds hurricanes in its grasp. Magic, though it promises happiness, gives testimony that the Hells—with all its power to cast men into shadows—cannot add one thing to the foul and deadly thing sin is. But Gate'har has cured men of their festering and putrid magic and saved them from a sinner's death, brought man upon the

Goddess's shoulders and sheltered them from the sin the magic men wield."

The crowd cheered in veneration at the cleric's sermon. His voice echoed through the streets as he stood on a small stage placed in front of the fountain sitting in the center of the square.

Carts, horses with riders, and merchants flowed past the spectacle as they went about their business. The compressed stench of men and women clouded the square as it mixed with dust from the horses and carts passing by.

Korrith shook his head at the sight and wished he had brought his cloak. He suddenly felt the need to hide, despite the warmth of the day. Although he had nothing to be ashamed of, the fact the preacher was insulting his abilities to cast magic, and drew a comparison to sinning, caused him to recoil into himself. The boisterous voice of the crowd, whipped into a religious fervor, compelled fear to crawl up his spine and prickle the hair at the base of his skull.

Hypocrite, he thought as he walked down the road away from the zealous crowd, who were still cheering the cleric's speech. *Gate'har priests use magic just as much as I do.*

He sighed with discontent as he threaded his way toward the general shop. *It was bad enough that mages were considered as lesser men and women,* he thought to himself. *But to have an entire religious sect as powerful as the Gate'har spreading dissidence is disgraceful.*

Korrith stopped outside of the shop and forced his hunched shoulders to relax. No one would know he was a mage unless he started casting spells in the streets. He had nothing to worry about, despite the feelings of guilt for being different. *Calm yourself, Korrith,* he told himself. He took a deep breath and let the tension drain away before stepping into the shop.

Korrith tossed the items he purchased onto the floor near the door, shutting it behind him as he entered the open floor home. The hearth was burning low in the stone pit. The spicy smell of something cooking in the pot hanging over the embers greeted him. The aroma and warmth of home melted away the fear and anger that had been clinging to him since he heard the clerics preaching.

He glanced toward Sorrna as she sat reading in a chair near the window. She peered up at him and smiled. The look faded, however, as Korrith's dour demeanor caught her attention.

"What happened?" she asked as she set the book down.

He walked over to the chair beside her and sat down before reciting the tirade he held witness to.

Sorrna shook her head in disgust. "Those clerics will have us hunted down and strung up before long," she said.

"They don't help any. Mages and the clerics are two sides to the same magic coin. You would think they would be on all our sides. Magic helps everyone, even the spells practiced by the priests," he said in dismay.

Sorrna put her book down on the small stand between them and stood up. She walked over to the cabinet next to the water basin and took out a clay pitcher and two pewter goblets, then returned to her seat. She set the items down on the table next to her book and poured the amber liquid into it. The smell of sweet spice filled the air.

"Here," she said, handing Korrith a goblet with some mead. "You're home now, it's over."

He took the offered drink and sipped it slowly. "I know. Thank you."

She watched him with an unguarded gaze, as if she was trying to probe his innermost thoughts.

"Dinner smells good," he said, the unease thawing on his shoulders like bricks of ice.

Sorrna smiled in appreciation.

"I'm starving," he said suddenly, his brow furrowing as he realized his stomach must have been screaming for some time.

"Well, it won't be ready for a few hours still. Maybe, though, I can think of something to keep your mind off of it and the rest of the woes you carry," Sorrna said. Her small, soft-featured face blushed slightly as she stood.

"Oh?" Korrith said, arching a brow at her.

Her skirt slipped down her legs to pool at her ankles, leaving only her long, white shirt to cover her body.

"Oh!" he grinned impishly.

She stepped out of the puddle of her dress and kneeled in front of him. She slid her small hands up his long legs to his crotch, where he knew she felt the growing warmth underneath his breeches.

"You spoil me," he said. "Again."

She grinned as her fingers worked the drawstring on his waist. "You'll have your chance to spoil me, several times."

Korrith closed his eyes and laid his head back against the chair. His thoughts melted away to this one moment, with her. Where everything in his world was alright.

Sorrna snuggled next to him, a hand settling on his heaving chest.

Korrith wrapped the arm she was lying on protectively around her shoulders. "I love you," he whispered.

"I love you too."

They lay on the bed, the familiar smell of their love permeating the air, mixed with the spicy smell of dinner hanging above the hearth. A look of contentment played across their faces.

"You get to take dinner off the hearth," Sorrna whispered against his naked body.

"Me?" he said huskily.

"Mmmm."

He chuckled and hugged her tighter, placing a kiss on her forehead. He enjoyed the feeling of her being near him. Her heated body, sticky with their love, pressed against his gave him comfort. It was something he would miss once he was on the road.

Chapter 4

DEPARTURE

SORRNA PEERED UP AT him, the edges of her blue eyes moist with unshed tears. He leaned over and kissed her lovingly.

They stood outside the southern gate to Xonthian City, where life flowed past them. They stared into each other's eyes as if they were trying to memorize their features, permanently etching the memory in their minds.

The horses Sengue Bebedor provided, currently anchored to an elegant carriage, stomped and snorted behind them, eager to be on the road. The chauffeur, a well-built man with fierce azure eyes, brown hair, and a matching beard, waited patiently in the driver's seat.

Sorrna took a deep, steadying breath.

"I have to go," Korrith said, caressing Sorrna's lips with a thumb.

"Be careful," Sorrna said. "Hurry home."

"I will," he replied, kissing her one more time before stepping up into the carriage. He gave her one last smile before closing the door.

She waved as the driver snapped the reins, prodding the horses to lurch forward. She blinked as the carriage pulled away, an unseen tear flowing down her cheek.

There was an odd, musty, old wooden smell to the carriage as Korrith sat down. It jolted forward, and he glanced around at the men sitting and talking idly.

"The little lady will be alright," Edrin said. "We'll be back before you know it."

"Yeah, I know," Korrith said. He shifted his attention to the man sitting beside Edrin, who had stopped talking to look at him. "I know we've met, but I don't believe we've been introduced. My name is Korrith," he said, offering his hand to the short, pudgy mage.

"Name's Jaal Moor," he said as he took Korrith's hand and shook it. His face was round with a large, pockmarked nose and two small, beady, grey eyes. Short amber hair spiked in all directions adorned his head.

The man's hand was sweaty. It took Korrith's entire will to keep from wiping it on his breeches. Instead, he smiled at Jaal, then turned to the man beside him.

"And you?" Korrith asked, holding his hand out to repeat the process.

The man took it and gave it a curt shake. "Von Sorka." The mage was just under Korrith's height, with brown hair neatly brushed back, crowning his average face. His features were stern and held an air of indifference.

"Pleasure, Von Sorka, Jaal," Korrith said as he sat back in the plush, cushioned seat of the carriage.

The interior was trimmed with red and beige pillows with matching curtains. The visible wood was carved in artistic swirls that dove in and out of other pieces as if they were made from a single tree, chiseled, and put back together. The wall opposite the door had a small cabinet with a wooden bar holding several crystal glasses and a decanter.

"Sengue must be a lord or something," Edrin said, studying around the cab as well. "Ever seen work this detailed?"

"No, I haven't," Korrith replied.

"I'm going to enjoy this journey," Von Sorka said. He removed a decanter from the cabinet and poured himself a glass. His narrow, dark amber eyes closed as he swallowed the contents.

Korrith shook his head. "If he is a lord, how come I've never heard of him?"

"Maybe he's from Xecutran? Or Juan'kij?" Edrin said with a shrug.

"Maybe," Korrith said, peering out the window as the farmland flowed by like water made of wheat.

"You worry too much, Korrith. Jaal, you want a drink?" Edrin said as he took the remaining glasses off the shelf, handing one each to Korrith and Jaal. "Remember when you couldn't recall the spell word for earth as we were trying to enchant that statue?"

Korrith laughed. "Gods, I do. I spent weeks looking through my books. I was starting to wonder if I ever knew the word at all."

"You were convinced you were going mad and that the word never even existed," Edrin said. He poured some of the pale brown liquid into each of their glasses, then set it back on the shelf.

"I remember waking up one night; it was, what, three in the morning? I pounded on your door yelling that I remembered. It had come to me while I was lying in bed worrying about it." Korrith laughed before taking a sip of the smooth, burning whiskey.

Edrin laughed, startling Jaal beside him. The two men laughed even more.

"This is going to be a long ride," Von Sorka muttered as he poured himself another dram of whiskey.

Korrith ignored the disdain from his neighbor. Shifting slightly, he settled farther back against a pillow next to him.

"Famous lord or not, he sure knows how to travel in style," Korrith said before taking another sip from his glass.

"Truer words have never been spoken," Edrin said, raising his glass in salute before downing the rest of his drink. "Who would have thought—lowly mages like us, traveling in luxury, getting paid good silver, and for what? Guarding a dead man?"

Korrith glanced out the window again. The farmlands were giving way to the forest. The uncultivated land sprouted fir trees, mixed with pine and the occasional oak.

Maybe Edrin was right. Maybe I was worried about nothing and every-thing would work out. It typically did, as Edrin pointed out, he thought to himself before finishing the contents of his glass. The trees became dense on his side of the carriage, making it feel as if the forest was going to swallow them.

The driver brought the carriage to a stop a few hours after the sun had set. The bearded man was untying the horses from the control arm of the carriage.

Korrith stepped out and groaned loudly as he stretched. His muscles loosened as blood flowed faster through his veins.

"Why'd we stop?" Edrin asked as he stepped out.

"To give the horses a rest," Von Sorka said as he pushed his way past Edrin. Jaal followed closely on his heels.

Korrith walked over to the chauffeur. "Need any help?"

"No, I got it," the man replied.

"We haven't been properly introduced. I'm Korrith, that's Edrin, Jaal, and Von Sorka," he said, pointing to the others briefly.

"Pleased to serve you. My name is Aarim. Now, if you don't mind, I have work to do."

Korrith nodded and left, giving him room to maneuver the horses to a nearby tree.

Edrin walked over and clapped Korrith on the shoulder. "Remember camping when we were kids? The smell of fire, the stars sparkling high above us in the heavens."

Korrith nodded, a smile spreading across his face. "I remember we lost you one time, had all our parents worried sick. I found you sitting in a creek, soaking wet, playing with the rocks," Korrith said.

"I was trying to stop the flow of water," Edrin said.

Korrith chuckled and climbed up to grab his and Edrin's bags from the top of the carriage. "Jaal, Von Sorka, you want yours while I'm here?"

"Yes, please," Jaal said, holding his hands up to wait for its delivery.

Korrith dropped it down to him, followed by Von Sorka's, then climbed back down.

"We'll set up camp there," Aarim said, pointing to a small pull out in the forest where a circle of stones had been placed.

The men set up camp and started a fire, giving Aarim time to tend the horses. By the time he was done, everything was ready for the evening meal to be prepared. Two rabbits were grilled on a spit, while a pot of potatoes boiled on a rock in the fire. Idle conversations grew quiet as the food was served and everyone became lost in the savory smell of roasting rabbit.

"That was delicious, Aarim," Korrith said as he tossed the last of the rabbit bones into the fire pit.

"Thank you, sir," the driver replied, taking a drink from his flask.

Korrith sat back against his pack and gazed at the stars above. His belly full, he started to doze off. As he approached the edge of slumber, he was awakened by the echo of footsteps. However, no one had moved from their places near the fire.

"Well, we have ourselves some travelers," a man said as the sound of steel sliding from its sheath hissed through the air.

Several men wearing a rag-tag assortment of patchwork armor appeared in the orange glow of the firelight. Swords, spears, and axes were held at the ready. Aarim stood quickly and made to draw his blade but was interrupted by the apparent leader of the bandits.

A large man with hulking muscles hit Aarim with the back of his fist, sending the driver sprawling to the ground.

"Now, let's try this civil-like," the leader said, pointing the sword tip at Aarim's throat. He wore slightly better armor than the rest, as if he had first choice when looting their victims.

"There's a chest 'ere, Wellis," a bandit near the carriage said.

Aarim tried to protest, but a swift boot from the leader, Wellis, quelled any uprising.

Von Sorka snarled and stood. Before the other men could point their spears at him, a gust of wind erupted from his outstretched fist. The force plowed into Wellis, knocking him backward and causing the bandit to lose his footing.

The other rouges dashed toward Von Sorka. Aarim, given room to breathe, tripped one of the bandits as they passed. He clawed his way to the man's chest. With a fluid motion, he took his boot knife from its hiding place and plunged it into the man's ribs.

"Mages!" the other bandits said in fear.

Wellis, stunned as he was, scrambled to his feet as Von Sorka approached. The mage's hand glowed fire red as he reached toward the bandit leader.

"I'll get you lot for this, mark my words," the bandit said as he retreated into the darkness, the rest of his men following behind.

Von Sorka let the flames dissipate into a snuffed spark, then returned to the campfire and sat back down.

Korrith watched in silence at the scuffle as his heart pounded loudly in his ears. Fear sent rivulets of sweat trickling down his back, and he was suddenly aware he had been useless. He glanced sidelong at Edrin, who cast his head down in reflected shame.

Chapter 5

PORT ORLYNNS

THE CITY OF PORT Orlynns held Xonthian's naval yards, as well as the second-largest warehouse district in the world. There were more ships in the harbor than there were on the ocean. Or at least, it seemed that way to Korrith.

A forest of masts dotted the bay as he climbed out of the carriage. The stench of decaying fish, mixed other unrecognizable odors, hung heavily in the air. The cry of seagulls sounded like shrill music. There was a chill breeze blowing in from the harbor, and the sky above them was grey. Wilderness loomed up around the city, hiding its size from his sweeping gaze.

The others climbed stiffly down from the carriage and stretched, while the driver untied their bags from the roof. He tossed them to the cobblestones with a loud thump. Jaal, who was the last to leave the carriage, flinched as a bag landed near his foot.

No one had mentioned the bandits since they attacked, and the remaining journey south had gone by with a thick air of unease. Even Korrith's heart skipped a beat as bags landed on the ground.

The chauffeur jumped down from his perch and handed the men a bag of silver each.

"Thank you, Aarim," Korrith said.

"This is your payment for this past week and the coming week's travel. You'll be paid the final amount upon your arrival back to Xonthian City. You'll stay the night here and meet the wagon with its cargo in the morning. Warehouse fifteen, at first light. Don't be late," Aarim said.

"Where's a good place to stay?" Edrin asked casually.

Aarim pointed down the road to a two-story building next to a stable and mumbled, "The Broken Wheel." Larger buildings sprang up behind it. Wood and stone homes clustered together farther south.

"Thank you again, Aarim," Korrith said as he picked his pack up.

The others followed suit and made their way to the inn. The cobblestone streets drove deeper into the heart of the city and along the bay. People lumbered in and out of the shops and stalls that lined the street, carrying various sacks and crates.

The four travel-weary men entered the inn, their eyes quickly adjusting to the dim candlelight. The Broken Wheel was an aged place, with smoke-stained windows and old wood that had seen its share of storms. The inside was clean, with several large tables and benches. The fireplace crackled lazily in the corner, opposite the stairs that likely led to the rooms above.

Korrith walked over to an empty table and sat down, tossing his pack on the floor beside him. Edrin sat on the bench with him, while Jaal and Von Sorka took up the opposite seat.

"Welcome to The Broken Wheel," a young, blonde woman said. Her dress flowed around her curvy body. Her face was pleasantly framed with curly black hair flowing to her shoulders. "What can I get for you gentle travelers?"

"Whatever's on the fire, and a mug of the city's specialty, please,"

Korrith said. "Do you have any rooms available?"

"Yes, we do, sir," the woman said with a smile.

"Good, good. A room as well please," Korrith said.

"Of course. And you?" the barmaid said, shifting her attention to Edrin.

"The same," Edrin replied, his eyes lingering on hers a little longer than was polite.

The other two ordered the same, with the exception of their drinks. Korrith and Edrin ordered Port Orlynns ale, Jaal ordered mead, and Von Sorka ordered straight whiskey. The woman returned a moment later with a book and quill, setting it down in front of Korrith. He recorded his name in the ledger and paid for his room.

"Thank you," she said, smiling at Edrin as he completed his signature.

"You're welcome," he said with a wink.

She giggled and slid the book to the next person. After everyone had finished signing in, Korrith nudged Edrin in the ribs.

"What?" he laughed.

"You'll get yourself in trouble, keep that up," Korrith said reprovingly.

Edrin waved a dismissive hand at this remark.

The barmaid returned a few moments later with their orders. She set a bowl of hot stew down in front of each of them, as well as their drinks.

"Thank you," Jaal said with a pleasant smile.

The woman winked at him, causing his skin to blush in response. "You're welcome, sweety."

Korrith laughed. "You have competition, Edrin."

"We'll see."

Jaal's blush deepened, causing the men to laugh uproariously.

"A book worm like him doesn't stand a chance," Von Sorka snickered.

"You're an archivist?" Korrith asked with a raised brow.

Jaal nodded.

Archivists were the keepers of knowledge for mages. It was a lonely job, or so Korrith had understood it to be. They were in charge of researching magic, how it worked. They were also a major source of new spells.

"Well, thank you for all you do," Korrith said with a raised glass.

"Can we get back to how *I'm* going to swoon the barmaid," Edrin asked with a wide grin.

The evening melted away with each round of drinks. Korrith excused himself and wandered upstairs to settle into his room after the third round. He was tired and wanted some peace and quiet. He was looking forward to not spending the night under the stars with four other men.

The room, much like the rest of the inn, was old and musty smelling, but also clean and well furnished. Korrith closed the door and set his pack down. The bed had a pine frame with a mattress that appeared to be stuffed with hay. It had forest green sheets and pillows, and the headboard was a tangle of branches. He sat down on the edge of the bed and sighed with relief.

He fell back onto the bed, kicking his boots off. *Tomorrow we need to report to the warehouse, then escort the sarcophagus to Xonthian City. What could possibly go wrong?* he thought. A thin smile spread across his lips before he drifted into a restful slumber.

Chapter 6

THEN THERE WERE THREE

Sorrna giggled in the warm sun as they built a sandcastle on the beach, even though waves kept washing it away. Korrith felt the frustration build with each new surge of water. Suddenly, there was a soft rapping sound, and he was back home, sitting at the table. Someone was knocking on the door. With a sharp realization, he awoke. The dark room of the inn surrounded him, filling his nostrils with the old, musty smell. A lump in Korrith's pillow dug into the side of his head, unnoticed until his consciousness stirred awake. The knock echoed through the room again, louder this time.

"Yes?" he called.

"This is your wakeup time, sir," a gentle voice said.

"Thank you," Korrith replied before groaning and sitting up. *Whose idea was it to get up this early?*

He stood and dressed reluctantly, opting to do so in a dark room rather than take time finding his flint to light a candle. Fully dressed, he threw his cloak on and headed downstairs. The other three men were waiting for him at the table where the barmaid from last night, looking tired and drained, was serving leftovers to them.

The group ate quietly, then departed. They traded the comfortable, warm interior of the inn for the cold, damp exterior. The empty streets made the city seem abandoned. The stars were still sparkling above them, but the moon was nowhere to be seen, giving the illusion they had stepped out into the abyss.

"Warehouse fifteen is this way," Edrin said as he led the group down a dark street a few yards from The Broken Wheel.

"How do you know that?" Korrith yawned.

"Carrie told me," Edrin said with a smile.

"Car- the barmaid?" Korrith asked, shooting him a glance.

Edrin laughed in response at Korrith's stunned expression.

Korrith laughed, too, and shook his head. They turned down another street, darker and narrower than the previous one. They could hear voices in the distance.

"Sounds like the docks aren't too far. This way," he said, leading them down a narrow alley.

They emerged into a small plaza surrounded by rundown homes and broken lean-tos. Lumps of sleeping vagrants snored from under wool blankets and other unidentifiable coverings used for warmth. On the other side, the plaza narrowed again, several alleyways branching off either side.

As they walked deeper into the darkness, the alley widened slightly. It became a road that ran along the backs of homes, as if it were designed for deliveries. The smell of human excrement mixed with the salty air from the bay was hard to ignore.

Before the mages could leave the dark road, several men stepped out of the shadows and barred their way. Korrith whirled in an attempt to retreat but saw there were more men behind them. At least eight altogether encircled them.

"Oi, look 'ere mates. Awfully early for merchants ta be roamin' around," a black-haired man said. He wore a wool skullcap around his head and ears, while leather armor covered his body.

The circle of men tightened. Steel flashed from sheaths, causing the four mages to draw closer together like trapped animals.

"Give us all your coin, an' we'll letcha live," the leader said. He was close enough Korrith could smell his rotten breath.

Jaal started to undo his pouch, but as he did, Von Sorka lifted his hand towrd the thief in front of him and spoke one word. With a reaction time born from years of training, the thief plunged his sword through the mage's chest, silencing the spell he was casting.

"Mages, huh?" the thieves' leader said.

Von Sorka clutched his wound and fell to the damp stone ground, blood pooling around him.

"Here, take it," Jaal said shakily.

"Aye, I will," the thief said as he yanked the coin purse from Jaal's hand.

Korrith and Edrin had untied their pouches and handed them to the thieves. Von Sorka's killer bent down and cut the purse from his corpse.

"Nice doing business with ya'," the thieves' leader said with a bow. They melted into the shadows, disappearing once again.

The three men stood there shaking from fear, adrenaline running through their veins.

"Wha-what do we do now?" Edrin asked as he peered down at Von Sorka's lifeless body.

"Let's go, nothing we can do," Korrith said.

"We can't just leave him," Edrin said.

"What would you have us do? Do we actually know him, his next of kin, anything?"

"Well, no."

"We'll tell someone at the warehouse. Maybe they will know Sengue and handle this. Come on, let's get out of here before they decide to come back."

Korrith guided them to the main thoroughfare. It was lined with several large, wooden buildings. The occasional dockworker could be seen in the distance, moving crates or other shipping containers.

"Anarchs," Edrin said finally, to everyone's unasked question.

"The thieves' guild?" Korrith asked, "I always thought they were a myth. Something the nobles told their children to scare them."

"They got rich off us," Edrin sighed.

Korrith nodded, although he was fine giving up his coin in exchange for his life. *No amount of silver was worth that*, he told himself.

Thoughts of Sorrna filled his mind as the weight of what occurred settled on him. The implications of what could have happened repeated in his mind like some macabre play. He shook away the horrifying images.

"We got lucky," Jaal said softly.

"Yeah," Edrin agreed.

The men walked to the warehouse district, where they could see the large network of piers stretching out into the gently lapping water. The black, tar-looking liquid undulating against the hulls of ships. Dock masters yelled out orders while men went about their jobs, oblivious to the murder that just happened nearby.

"There," Edrin said, pointing to a wooden warehouse a few yards away. The number fifteen was painted on the side near the sliding barn doors.

The men made their way inside to find a burly man standing near a wagon, where he was lashing a rope to the tie-downs.

"We're here about a sarcophagus," Korrith said to the man, who peered up at them as they approached.

"Aye, this is it right here," the man said, his dirty, calloused hand smacking the black stone container on the back of the wagon.

The sarcophagus was nearly as dark as the sky outside. The light from the braziers burning in the warehouse allowed Korrith to make out intricate symbols carved into the stone. He didn't recognize any of the markings that wrapped themselves around the lid, as if they were meant to hold whatever was inside down.

A younger man, not much older than Korrith, stepped from behind crates littering the warehouse and greeted the three men jovially. He wore dark red robes and a black cloak. He had piercing grey eyes and black hair that was tied up in a ponytail. "My name is Sloan, a pleasure to meet you. I work for Sengue Bebedor. I hope your journey was easy."

Edrin scoffed.

Korrith explained their encounter with the Anarchs and where Von Sorka's corpse could be found. Edrin added a quick explanation of running into the bandits outside of Xonthian City.

Sloan shook his head in dismay. "I will see to the body. Now, if you don't mind, I don't have a lot of time left this morning to explain what you need to do."

Korrith arched a brow at Sloan's casual dismissal but said nothing. *What could he say?* he thought. The concerns and doubt that plagued him since leaving Xonthian City wormed their way back into his mind.

Sloan climbed into the bed of the wagon and caressed the sarcophagus lovingly.

"All you three need to do is place a hand on the seal here," Sloan said as he demonstrated. "Your connection to the flow of magic will renew the spell. Until we can get this into a permanent home, of course."

"We'll get it to Xonthian City," Korrith said.

Sloan nodded and jumped down. "I must go now. You three have a safe journey," he said as he disappeared deeper into the warehouse.

"Let's get going," Edrin said. "I'm starting to agree with you, Korrith."

"About what?" Korrith asked as he climbed up into the driver's seat of the wagon.

Edrin sat beside him while Jaal took up an empty spot next to the sarcophagus in the wagon bed. "Something doesn't feel right."

Korrith pursed his lips as he studied his friend. He turned his attention toward the horses strapped to the wagon. He gave a click with his tongue and snapped the reins gently. The fear and suspicions he had during the trip south flooded back, causing his heart to race as if it was trying to outrun the panic.

Chapter 7

◆─○─◆

THE ROAD HOME

*T*HREE DAYS. THAT'S IT. *Just three more,* Korrith thought to himself as he sat next to the sarcophagus.

The road was hard packed from decades of traffic consisting of carts, horses, and people. The horse hooves pounding into the earth drummed through his ears, to the point he heard them when he slept. The air was crisp, and the weather had cleared once they left the forests around Port Orlynns. It was no longer grey and wet.

"Hey, Edrin, pull over. I need to piss," Korrith said.

"Yeh," he replied. He pulled back on the reins, slowing the team of horses until they came to a full stop on the side of the road.

Korrith climbed out and stretched. Edrin set the reins down and climbed from the driver seat, where Jaal joined them.

Korrith walked over to a tree a few feet away and relieved himself, then tied his breeches with the drawstring.

When he turned toward the wagon, he saw the sarcophagus glistening in the sunlight. Edrin, who was a few feet away from him, grunted and tied his pants closed before stepping beside Korrith.

"What are you looking at?" Edrin asked, wiping his hand on his pant leg.

"Do you see that?"

Edrin studied the stone coffin and shrugged.

"You don't see the aura?" Korrith asked, his brow furrowing. "As if the thing was hot, you know, like the cobblestones do when it's warm out."

"No, I don't," Edrin said.

"I don't see it either. But... Have you not felt yourselves become drained faster?" Jaal interjected from behind them.

Korrith jerked away with a start; he had forgotten the quiet man was even there.

"Now that Jaal mentions it, I have noticed that. You don't suppose it's that thing, do you?" Edrin said.

Korrith pondered the question. He knew enchantments could be made to trigger when the presence of mages were around, but typically that took some sort of incantation on the part of the mage to set off. Then there was the smell, like when lightning strikes the earth.

"Jaal's right. If that's the case, there are levels of magic I can't comprehend."

"What are we transporting?" Edrin asked.

"A dead man. Although that doesn't explain what we feel draining us. I just don't know."

"Let's get going. The sooner we get this over with, and paid, the better," Edrin said as he climbed back up to the driver's seat. He took the reins in his gloved hands and waited for the others to climb aboard.

"I'm not sure I even care about the money anymore," Jaal said, sitting down beside Edrin.

After being robbed in Port Orlynns, they wouldn't earn nearly the amount they were originally promised. Korrith couldn't disagree with Jaal. He just wanted to get home, alive. He sat down and scooted as far away from the stone sarcophagus as he could. Edrin snapped the reins, and they were once again moving toward Xonthian City.

Chapter 8

TRAPPED

TIRED, DRAINED, AND SICK of the road's constant droning of hooves and wheels, the three men were glad when the trees began to thin out. Farmlands spread out in front of them, marking the outskirts of Xonthian City.

Korrith spurred the horses unintentionally faster, causing his friend to be jostled and tossed about. Realizing Edrin was yelling at him to slow down, he pulled back on the reins and brought the horses to an even pace that didn't cause the wagon to rattle around.

"Gods, Korrith, Xonthian City isn't going anywhere," Edrin said, rubbing his shoulder after he hit it when he bounced against the rail.

Korrith looked at Jaal, who was slouched on the bench with black, puffy rings under his eyes. They had to stop each night to allow the horses some respite from the drive north. The men found ample time to sleep, but the act had become restless, and there was no refreshment from it. They awoke each morning feeling drained and tired, as if they had spent the last week wide awake.

Korrith shifted his attention back to the road. The large stone pillars of the South Gate loomed in front of them. They checked in with the guards and, once they were cleared, made their way toward the cemetery on the northeastern edge of the city.

"I'll be glad when this is over," Korrith said tiredly.

"Me too," Edrin replied.

Jaal nodded but said nothing.

The main road, where the Stone Flame was located, forked to the right toward the slums. Korrith prodded the horse in that direction, and once they reached the slums, he turned left onto a winding road that ran north toward Saints Hill and the cemetery.

"Hey, we're going to pass your house," Endrin chuckled, although there was no humor in his eyes. They remained dull and tired looking.

Korrith nodded and watched as the house came into view. He wanted to rid himself of this sarcophagus before he saw Sorrna. He couldn't stand it if he caused her harm.

As they passed by the house, the wagon lurched violently, sending Edrin flying across the road. He rolled in the dirt and landed in the brush a few yards away. The horses protested and came to a stop as a wagon wheel snapped off, sending the axle digging into the dirt.

Jaal gripped the driver seat. His hands—slick with moisture—lost their hold and sent him sliding off the end onto the ground. He rolled away just as horse hooves stomped heavily beside him.

Korrith yanked on the reins, trying to bring the horses under control. Dust thrown up from the accident billowed around them, like fog rolling in from the ocean. He leapt from the wagon, calmed the horses, then made sure Jaal and Edrin were ok. Jaal was already standing next to the broken wagon, brushing himself off. Edrin was limping toward them. Blood was running down his right arm and face where he had hit the dirt and skidded to a stop.

"Edrin, you okay?" Korrith asked as he walked over to him.

"Yeh, I'll be fine," he said, placing a tentative hand on his brow where the skin had been ripped away by the dirt. "How bad does it look?"

"Doesn't look deep," Korrith replied as he glanced at the broken wheel.

A crowd had gathered to watch, including Sorrna, who saw Korrith and ran over to him.

"Oh, hon!" she said, throwing her arms around him and hugging him tightly.

"Sorrna!"

"I heard the crash and came out to investigate," she said with a smile, which faded when she saw the weary, pale features of his dirt-stained face.

"We need to get this out of here," he said, pushing her away.

She protested but must have seen he was genuinely scared. His attention fell on the crowd, pointing at the stone coffin. The sarcophagus had broken loose, and because the wagon was now lying sideways on the axle, the lid had slid off.

Edrin and Korrith drew closer, while Jaal walked around the back of the wagon, his eyes fixed on the container.

As they approached, the man inside opened his eyes, causing the three mages to jump back. The creature moved and pushed the lid the rest of the way off.

"A litch," Jaal said with a shaky voice. "This is a litch!"

Edrin and Korrith exchanged fearful expressions. Korrith whirled around and yelled at the crowd to disperse. But it was too late; the creature was free, and no one was heeding his warning. Sorrna glanced around in panic. The onlookers, enraged by the sight of magic, started to hurl stones at them. One of them caught Korrith in the forehead, and he stumbled back. A thin line of blood ran down his face, a warning that things were escalating quickly. As much as she tried, Sorrna could do nothing to quell the sudden flow of anger from the crowd.

The creature stood, matching Korrith's full height, and rocks went unnoticed as they bounced harmlessly off its skeletal frame. Its dull, grey skin and sunken black eyes moved unnaturally as it took in its surroundings. It wore clean, black cloth robes that appeared as if they were new.

"If this thing gets to the graveyard, it'll have an army of undead at its disposable," Edrin said.

"Then we kill it!" Korrith said as he summoned a flame in his hand.

The crowd behind him began to scream, realizing they were about to witness a magic battle that would be unaffected by their stone tossing. Yet still they remained, fixated by the horror of the creature. *As if the undead creature shambling out of a coffin wasn't a warning enough*, Korrith thought bitterly, clenching his teeth.

Edrin followed suit and summoned fire in the palm of his hand.

"Jaal, move out of the way," Korrith said.

Jaal looked at him, mouth agape and sweat visible on his pallid skin. Before he could comprehend Korrith's command, the litch reached over and grabbed Jaal by the throat, causing the mage to gasp in fear. His hands tore feebly at the litch's tight grasp as his eyes widened in horror.

"Damn it," Korrith said. "Take it down, Edrin!"

"But, Jaal."

"It's either him or all of us if it raises the dead from the cemetery," Korrith replied.

The two remaining mages stretched their hands out toward the litch, and balls of flame shot at the undead creature. A howl of pain and terror escaped Jaal as the fire erupted around him and the creature. The flames grew, intensifying to a near-blue haze. The horses reared, causing the sarcophagus to fall to the road. No longer weighed down by the coffin, they were able to drag the wagon away despite the broken wheel.

The smell of burning flesh billowed in thick, black clouds around them. Many of the onlookers gave in to their fear and ran off. Others, frozen in terror, dropped the rocks from their hands.

"One more time," Korrith called out. He made a sign in the air with his hand and whispered the incantation for fire. A ball of flames sprang to life in his palm, and he once again threw it at the creature.

This intensified the fire already engulfing the creature, causing the heat to grow in magnitude and force the onlookers back, less they risk being burned.

Jaal's body went limp, and he no longer screamed as his skin boiled and flaked off in large clumps. The litch, too, showed signs of burning away. It's once-grey skin was now black, and its eyes had evaporated before the mages hit it with a second fireball. After several tense seconds, the creature fell forward, once again lifeless. The flames continued to burn, sending putrid smoke streaking through the late afternoon sky.

A yell shattered the crackling air, and Korrith spun around to see a dozen men encircling them. They were not the city guard, however. As bad as that would have been, what greeted him was far worse.

"No," Korrith shouted, clenching his fists.

"By the gods. Who?" Edrin asked. He turned to see several townsmen waving sharpened axes and scythes.

It wasn't their sudden appearance that caused Korrith's fear and anger. The cleric he had seen weeks ago giving a sermon in the town square held Sorrna tightly with muscular arms, a dagger resting under her chin.

"You sinful magi," the cleric said with an air of indignation. "You will repent your ways for the evil you have brought to our home."

"We'll do whatever you want, please," Korrith said quickly. "Just let her go; she has nothing to do with this."

The cleric buried his face in Sorrna's hair an inhaled deeply. A wicked smile split the cleric's lips. "She smells of foul magic."

"Don't worry, Korrith. I've got this," Edrin said wearily.

"No! Don't—"

Edrin grinned and walked into the half-circle of bandits, his hands held up in surrender. "I learned a new trick; want to see?" He dropped his hands as if he were slamming them down on a table. Fire erupted in a crescent around him that fanned toward the mob, engulfing their legs from the knees down. The force of the eruption knocked them off their feet. Edrin turned his attention to the remaining man, who stood behind him. As he did, the farmer's blade pierced Edrin's chest. He gasped in pain as blood ran down his torso, then his leg, and pooled at his feet. He fell to his knees, clasping a hand to the wound.

"Well, that was- I'm sorry to say this, friend. But your buddy there, he only made things worse," the cleric said as he slid the dagger along Sorrna's throat.

A ribbon of blood streamed black down her neck as she gasped and fell to her knees. Her hands clasped her throat.

"No!" Korrith yelled.

It was as if Korrith's rage and frustration fed the globe of fire in his outstretched hand. It grew in intensity with every passing heartbeat. Blood dripped down his face, coloring his already blurred vision red.

"I've had it! Your hatred will end here," Korrith growled as he flicked his hand toward the onlookers. The orb of fire elongated as it flew through the air before hitting the holy man.

The explosion that followed shook the hills. Windows shattered in nearby houses as the power of the flames washed over crops and homes like a red and orange wave. The cleric took the brunt of Korrith's wrath and exploded into red mist before evaporating in the heat. The onlookers were frozen with fear in the path of his rage. Engulfed bodies screamed and howled in pain before falling to the scorched earth, charred and lifeless.

"No more hatred," he whispered. His eyes scanned the carnage, tears mixing with the blood on his face. Korrith ran over to Sorrna's slumped body and fell to his knees. He pulled her to him and rocked her in his lap as the fires around him raged. He bowed his head and added, "What have I done?"

Chapter 9

GARDEN OF THE DEAD

B RANCHES SWAYED ABOVE KORRITH as the tree danced peacefully in the breeze. He no longer smelled the raw earth under him, having grown used to its musty stench days ago. The air around him was cool under the brush of the cemetery where he lay. Very few people visited the dead. The area was densely populated by bushes and places to hide.

Korrith rolled onto his side, pulling his cloak tighter around him. He glanced at Edrin, who was growing paler with each passing day. He had bandaged the wound the best he could with the materials he could scrounge up. He watched over him, forgoing sleep in exchange for making sure his friend rested and healed. He only slept when it was unavoidable. When he did risk closing his eyes, he saw Sorrna's lifeless body in his arms. Her visage, once filled with life and promise, stared back at him with cold reflection.

We had to run, he told himself again. It had become his mantra.

Sorrna, having had no money, no next of kin, and a murderer for a lover, was not given a burial. Instead, her body was burned in a pyre with the rest of the dead from that day.

"I'm sorry," he whispered to her ghost. *Another mantra*, he thought bitterly.

He tossed back around to peer up at the sky. The early morning sun began to spread its pink and red fingers like a ghostly hand brushing away the blackness of the night.

Korrith knew they couldn't stay in the cemetery forever, sleeping among the dead. He couldn't hide there the rest of his miserable life. He sat up and glanced around the empty cemetery. Rows of headstones rolled down along the hillside, the occasional mausoleum taking up large patches of earth.

"Edrin?" he whispered. "We need to get moving."

His friend stirred awake, nodded, then winced in pain.

Korrith helped Edrin stand, and once his friend was stable, he picked up his pack and slung it over his shoulder. He pulled his hood up over his dirty, bearded face. Edrin did the same. They were lucky that when the horses had run during the commotion they had stopped near the road to the cemetery. They were able to collect their packs as they ran past. Its contents afforded them a few days of food and water—something they had rationed closely over the last week.

They walked cautiously toward the large stone gate that exited to the city's northwestern side. Korrith slipped into the shadows cast down by the arch and peered out onto the main road. It was still early, and there was very little foot traffic. They walked slowly and carefully along the road toward his house, choosing to stick to the shadows of homes as much as possible.

He didn't know what they were going to do or where they would go. *The reasonable place to start,* he thought, *was home. Like most journeys, home is where you begin.*

As they drew closer, he saw the scarred earth and broken homes that were shattered when he killed the cleric. The fire spread beyond his vision and, in the end, had engulfed half the eastern edge of the city, including the slums.

Korrith sighed and shook his head. He studied the house he had spent most of his adult life in. It was crumbling, shattered, and looted.

"Think... Think there's anything left?" Edrin asked softly.

"No, I don't," Korrith replied as they entered.

The interior was ransacked and torn to pieces. Korrith walked to the kitchen and opened the cupboards. Inside was half of loaf of hard bread. A jug of wine lay on the floor, its contents staining the floorboards black as if shadows had been permanently etched there. He walked over to the bed and sat down, bowing his head in shame.

Edrin sat quietly in a chair he had righted and watched Korrith silently.

"We could run. Maybe disappear in a small town like North Kelsa," Edrin said finally.

"And what about you?" Korrith snapped. "You'll never make it that far."

Edrin looked at him blankly.

"I'm sorry, you didn't deserve that," Korrith said finally. He pulled some of the sheets from the bed and made bandages for Edrin. "Take your shirt off."

"I'm not that kind of fella, you know that," Edrin said with a weak smile.

"I need to change your bandages, you dolt," Korrith said, trying to force amusement into his words, although he wasn't sure he succeeded.

Edrin removed his shirt, allowing Korrith to peel away the makeshift bandages. They stuck to his fiery red skin, causing the wound to bleed again.

Korrith folded some of the muslin sheet to staunch the flow of blood. He tore several long strips to wind around Edrin's chest to keep the thick, wadded pad against the wound.

"There, that's better. I wish I has some hard alcohol to clean it with," Korrith said. He stood and paced the dust- and debris-strewn room when he heard a commotion outside. Korrith heard armor jingling, and it was drawing close.

"How'd they find us so fast?" Edrin asked.

Panic shot through Korrith's body, igniting the adrenaline in his veins. He darted to the door and risked a glance.

"They here for us?" Edrin whispered.

Korrith held a hand up to his lips, indicating silence.

Eight city guards, wearing polished chain mail with steel breastplates and carrying pikes, rattled their way toward his house. As they reached the path leading to it, the soldiers continued on to the home beside his. He heard them crash through the front door, and a second later, a woman screamed.

Korrith watched the guards pull a half-dressed woman from the home. Sheets billowed around her as she tried to hold them to her breasts and fight off the guards at the same time. There was yelling from inside the house. Her husband appeared to also be fighting the guards.

"By the king's orders, his Royal Highness has declared all mages enemy of the state," the guard's leader said, holding a roll of parchment up and reading from it.

"I'm not a mage!" the women screamed as one of the guards hefted her over his shoulder.

"She is not a mage! Listen to her, please," the husband cried as he clawed at the guards. One of those he was pleading with punched him, sending him reeling to the ground.

The guards marched back toward the castle, their captive slung over a shoulder like a sack of grain.

Korrith melted back into the shadows of his home as they passed by. His mind raced at the implications; not only had he killed innocent people because of his rage and anger, but he had doomed all mages.

"We need to get out of the city," Edrin whispered, sweat beading on his forehead.

Korrith only nodded in response.

Chapter 10

FEVER OF HATE

They waited until the sun had dropped below the horizon before leaving the shadows of his former, broken-down home. With one last backward glance, he left the place that had been his refuge with Sorrna.

They crept through the burnt remains of the slums. Finally reaching the main road leading to the city's Eastern Gate, they turned west toward the heart of the city.

"We could head east and disappear into the forest a few miles away. Or we could go west, steal some horses and head to North Kelsa," Korrith said as he glanced at his friend, who was hugging his wound.

"Either choice we make, we would need to find or steal provisions," Edrin said weakly. "I may not make it to North Kelsa on horseback."

"We can't stand here all day," Korrith whispered. "Come on. You're right, we need supplies."

Korrith led them west, back toward the city center. The city was beginning to stir. Workers mulled about the street to begin their daily chores. The two mages went unnoticed, appearing to the casual onlooker as beggars stumbling through the streets.

As they crossed the city's canal, which ran the length of the farmland outside of town, larger homes and businesses replaced the crowded city squares. People clogged the streets. They carried various farming tools, hammers, spades, and an occasional sword or two that had seen better days.

"What is this-" Edrin started to ask, but was cut short as the crowd began to chant.

"No more magi! No more murder!" the throng of people yelled in unison.

Edrin stumbled as he ran into one of the protesters.

"Hey, watch it scumbag. What's wrong with you?" the man growled.

Korrith bowed. "So sorry, sir," he said, pulling Edrin away.

They melted into the shadows of a nearby building and watched the mob march north, toward the castle. Demands for justice, vile hatred, and unfiltered curses floated through the air.

"We didn't do anything," Edrin whispered, wiping sweat from his face with the back of a hand.

"We did," Korrith said softly. "We did do something. We brought a litch into the city. We killed people with magic."

Edrin sighed and shook his head in shame.

The man Edrin had bumped into repeatedly glanced back over his shoulder at them, making Korrith uncomfortable. "We need to move," he said.

Korrith led Edrin farther down the road, away from the mob, unaware several members of the crowd broke off and followed them. Weapons waved maliciously in the air, their wielders eager to find someone to use them on.

"Hey!" their leader called.

Korrith snapped his head around and saw the men approaching, pulling Edrin faster along the road. "Come on, we need to move."

"I said stop!" the man yelled.

Korrith concentrated on escaping their stalkers. He reached the conclusion they might need to use magic. *The irony of that*, he thought bitterly.

Korrith guided Edrin into a shadowed alleyway and quickly pressed him up against the wall. He whispered for him to be quiet as he cast a spell to conceal them. When the mob came into view, all they saw was an empty passage.

"I knew I recognized that bearded fella," the man leading the mob said. "That's the one I seen, kill all them folk in the slums."

"They must have used magic and vanished," one of the other men said. "Come on, we need to find them!"

The mob yelled in agreement and ran down the alley, oblivious they passed mere inches from their prey.

"That was close," Edrin whispered.

Korrith dispersed the illusion, sweat trickling down his forehead. He was breathing heavily at the exertion.

"Are you ok?" Edrin asked.

"I'll be fine. Let's get out of here," Korrith said, leading them back to the main road.

They walked in silence, each lost in their thoughts and the grim reminder that the odds were stacked against them, heavily.

"Sengue must have wanted this," Korrith said finally.

Edrin glanced at him sidelong, a question on his pale face.

"The people were already angry at magic users," Korrith said. "We were already hated for our abilities, our differences."

Edrin shrugged, wincing with the movement. "We... We're different, sure, but we're still humans. We're still people."

"All they see is our differences; that's it," Korrith said bitterly. "Sengue must have known that. And that all it would take for people to riot in the streets was a spark."

Edrin stopped and fixed him with a stern gaze. "He wouldn't have known what we would do."

Korrith looked down, then away. "What we would do? We did exactly what that litch would have done. He would have killed a countless number of innocent people," he said softly.

"I don't blame you. Not one bit," Edrin said.

"I lost control."

"We were tired and drained from that damn sarcophagus," Edrin added.

Korrith pursed his lips and started walking again. They passed the Stone Flame, and once again the streets became filled with people. Unlike the mob previously, this was traffic from merchants, travelers, and the occasional noble.

The main street created a cross in the center of the city that ran in the four directions of the compass. A large fountain stood in the middle of the road, where water bubbled up in the basin. The Stone Flame sat on the northeast corner of the square.

Korrith took a step toward the market that sat opposite of the Stone Flame when something caught his eye.

Sitting behind the tavern was Sengue's carriage. The dark, carved wood was unmistakable.

"Well, by the gods," Korrith said.

"Wait, where-" Edrin started to say as he followed behind his friend.

The companions entered the Stone Flame and saw Aarim, the bearded carriage driver, sitting at a table. He glanced up just as the two men approached and sat down as if they were invited. Aarim's eyes widened briefly, then settled back behind a mask of indifference.

"Where's Sengue?" Korrith demanded.

The barmaid came over to see if the new arrivals needed a drink, but Korrith shot her a glower, causing her to back away in rejection.

"That wasn't very nice," Aarim said, taking a swig from his mug.

"Where is Sengue?" Korrith repeated.

"Not here, if that's what you're wanting to know," the bearded driver said, glancing between the two men. "Your friend doesn't look well."

Korrith ignored the statement. "We need a ride to North Kelsa. You're going to give us one."

Aarim arched a brow in response.

"You will take us there, in the carriage, after you buy enough provisions for us to survive the trip," Korrith said, low and with as much menace as he had ever heard come from his own voice.

"You know what we're capable of," Edrin added.

Aarim paused as if weighing his options, then nodded. "Fine, meet me out back."

"No," Korrith said. "We'll stay right here while you order from the barmaid and pay for it, and we'll leave together." Korrith peered at Aarim levelly and saw a snarl twitch at the edge of his lip.

"Fine," Aarim said, raising a hand to summon the barmaid.

Chapter 11

FALSE CROWN

KORRITH AND EDRIN FOLLOWED Aarim to the carriage. Korrith's pack was full of food and two skins of water. Edrin winced as he climbed up to the cabin and fell onto the cushions, a hiss of pain escaping his lips.

"Your friend may not survive the trip," Aarim said as he fastened the last horse in place.

"He'll be fine. Just get us as far away from here as possible," Korrith said as he climbed up into the carriage and closed the door.

"You should just leave me," Edrin said.

"No, I'm not losing anyone else." He opened his pack and took out a skin of water, pressing it to his friend's lips. "Drink."

Edrin drank the water, only stopping when Korrith moved it away.

"Easy, friend, we need to be careful," Korrith said, putting the stopper back in the spigot before replacing the flask in his pack.

The carriage rolled forward onto the cobblestone road. Korrith peered out of the curtains and saw the main square pass by. The carriage turned left and headed toward the Southern Gate.

"We'll be out of the city before long, Edrin. We'll get somewhere safe, and then find you some help," Korrith said, studying his pale, sweating friend. "Hang on."

Edrin smiled weakly, relaxing deeper into the cushioned seat of the carriage.

Korrith felt the change of the road's surface. He knew he would find the plains surrounding the city and the farmlands situated there.

"I'm sorry."

"Sorry for what?" Korrith asked as he rubbed his weary face.

"For getting you into this. It's my fault you're here," Edrin said softly.

Korrith shook his head slowly. "No, it's not. You didn't force me to come along when the job was offered. I did that; I accepted the job."

Edrin moaned in response. His eyes were closed, and pain twisted his face.

"Hang on," Korrith repeated. Edrin didn't respond; he had slipped into unconsciousness.

Korrith focused on Edrin. Having assured himself his friend was still alive, he sat back, realizing his heart had been racing tensely. He forced himself to calm down and took a deep, leveling breath.

Several minutes went by before Korrith blinked hard, trying to keep himself from relaxing too much. He leaned forward and looked out the window to see the farmlands were still passing by, as they had a few weeks ago. *We have come full circle,* he thought to himself dryly.

Korrith sat back as the droning of the wheels on the hard-packed earth melted away to white noise. The gently rocking carriage lulled him into closing his tired and weary eyes with a promise that when he opened them again, they would be safe.

He thought of better times not long ago, and as he slipped further into the void of sleep, he no longer had control over his thoughts. Peaceful dreams grew to nightmares the further into the void of unconsciousness he slipped. People were chasing him, and every time he glanced around for help, they would fade away. Then he was drowning, and the water around him turned to blood as he slipped below the surface. Edrin was there, staring at him with wide, milky eyes, his face pale and motionless.

Korrith's eyes flew open in panic as he realized they were no longer moving. "Edrin, wake up," he whispered.

Edrin stirred, fixing him with a weary expression.

There were voices outside the carriage, but he couldn't make out what was being said. Korrith slid a hand up to the red curtain and pushed it aside.

As he peered out, the blood in his veins turned to ice, and he stopped breathing for an instant. He saw Xonthian Castle and several city guards surrounding the carriage with weapons drawn.

"What... What is it?" Edrin whispered as he strained to sit up.

"We've been betrayed," Korrith growled.

Edrin tried to peer through the window but instead slid weakly into the sweat-soaked cushions.

"We're back in Xonthian City. Aarim has taken us in a circle!" Korrith said, anger flaring in his veins, thawing them.

"I don't want to die in prison," Edrin said weakly. "Don't let them take me."

Korrith shot him a glance. "What are you-" he started to ask but was cut short.

"Come out peacefully, or we'll be forced to use whatever means necessary to get you out, dead or alive," one of the guards yelled.

"Come here, please," Edrin said, his eyes closed tightly in pain.

Korrith did as asked, sliding next to his friend.

Edrin took the dagger from Korrith's belt and handed it to him, shaking.

"No!" Korrith said vehemently. "I won't. Maybe there is a cleric who can-"

"Do you... Do you really think they will give us quarter after what we did?" Edrin asked, looking up at his friend with tears streaming down his dirt-stained face. "Please... Please don't let them take me like this. It's over, Korrith. Just... Just let me go."

Korrith wiped away his own tears. They sat in silence, their hands clasped over the hilt of the dagger. Their eyes pleaded; Korrith's for forgiveness and Edrin's giving it.

Together they moved the dagger, the tip hanging over Edrin's chest like a falling arrow.

"Thank you," Edrin whispered as the blade slid silently into his breast, slipping between the ribs and piercing his heart. Edrin let out a long, relieved sigh as his last breath wheezed its way from his lungs.

"I'm sorry," Korrith said as Edrin's hands slipped lifelessly from the dagger's hilt. He repeated his mantra again as the door to the carriage was flung open and he was pulled out.

Chapter 12

◄─○─►

TRUTH HAS CONSEQUENCES

Rats scurried just out of his sight as he sat in the dark, dank cell. The floor was hard and filthy, layered with mud and other less desirable matter. The stench of human excrement permeated the air as it mixed with fear and blood. The prison cell was the size of a large closet and had only a steel pin above his head, in the wall, which currently held the chains that bound his wrists.

Another prisoner wailed in the darkness, the type of moaning that droned on for hours. There was clanging mixed in as if the jailers were playing processions with steel and wood, and the choir was the screams of the tortured.

Korrith shifted the weight of the iron chains. His wrists were rubbed raw. Blood trickled down to his elbows, dripping soundlessly to the mud-covered stone of the cell floor.

Footsteps echoed through the iron slots in the thick wood door, followed by the sound of a key turning the tumbler with a heavy clank. The door to his cell opened, and a wave of nauseating orange torchlight flooded the room.

"Sorry to keep you waiting. We're a bit backed up with all the magi comin' through here lately." The jailer grinned. He was large and missing several teeth. His skin glistened with sweat, caked-on blood mixed in.

Korrith could tell he wasn't sorry as he unlocked his chain from the wall and dragged him to his feet.

"Come on, we got some questions for ya," he said. His breath was hot and smelled worse than the prison cell.

Korrith was pulled along like a dog on a chain as he was led out of the cell and down the torch-lit hallway. Screams and moans of pain drifted from the other cells as they passed.

He was led to a large room with a brazier in the center. Several iron pokers lay in the coal, their handles protruding from the flames like fingers. Horrific chairs, tables, and spiked implements sat around the room—stained black with blood.

A cleric of Gate'har stood near one of the chairs with leather restraints. He was reading from a book and looked up when the two men approached.

"Ah, you are Korrith," the cleric said. "Please, have a seat."

The jailer chuckled mockingly as he walked Korrith over to the thick wooden chair. He pushed him down and fastened the leather straps around his limbs once his hands were freed from the iron manacles.

"Now then, Korrith, we- I have some questions for you. Each question must be answered truthfully. If my friend here detects a lie, we'll have to resort to pain. And pain can be a great motivator for telling the truth," the cleric said with an impish grin.

The jailer walked over to the fire and shifted the steel rods in the coal, as if testing them. The smell of smoke was thick in the air and mixed with the sweet putrid stench of burned flesh.

"Let's start off with a simple question. You are Korrith Borne, correct?" the cleric asked.

"Yes," Korrith replied softly.

The cleric nodded in agreement; he set the book down and scribbled in it. "Good, good. Now then, you are accused of torching nearly half of western Xonthian. Killing a cleric, as well, it appears in these reports. Is that also correct?"

Korrith bowed his head in shame. "Yes."

"Witnesses say that you also brought a litch into the city, and that it attacked you. That must have been embarrassing. Was it your plan to release the litch?" the cleric asked.

"No, we didn't bring- no, wait!" Korrith broke off as the jailer turned around, holding a poker. The tip of it was glowing white-hot.

"I warned you not to lie," the cleric said, exasperated.

The large jailer held the poker against the back of Korrith's hand, causing the mage to scream in agony. His flesh sizzled and popped, and the smell that followed was sickly.

"Let's try again. Was it your plan to bring the litch into town?" the cleric asked again.

"Y-yes, b-but we didn't know," Korrith said, forcing down nausea from the pain. "We were hired."

The cleric studied him for a moment, then wrote something in his book. The jailer set the poker in the fire and shifted back to Korrith, a knife in his hand. He slit the mage's clothes open, exposing his heaving, sweaty chest.

"Who hired you?" the cleric asked.

"S-Sengue Bebedor."

"I told you not to lie," the cleric said, nodding to the jailer, who picked up another iron poker.

The tip pressed into Korrith's breast, eliciting a scream of pain. Stars jumped around his vision as it contracted.

"You were not hired," the cleric sighed.

Korrith tried to make sense of the comment. *They were hired, Sengue hired them. He was...* His thoughts trailed off.

"Where are the other mages?" the cleric asked.

Korrith tried to push the pain away as his brain, muddled and confused as it was, tried to form coherent thoughts. The only question he could grasp onto as they fluttered past was: Why did Aarim turn them in?

"Where are the other mages?" the cleric repeated.

"W-what other m-mages?" Korrith said. He was trying to stall; the answer had to be somewhere in his confused, pain-riddled head.

"We know there is a consortium of mages here in Xonthian City. Where are they?" the cleric asked again, irritated.

Korrith glanced up at him; he had his answer. Like getting caught in a cold rain, fear trickled down his back in rivulets. *Aarim, no, Sengue had used him as a martyr*, Korrith thought bitterly.

His face, already white from the pain and terror of being tortured, blanched further.

"Well?" the cleric asked.

"I... I don't know," Korrith said a moment before the hot iron scorched his skin. He screamed in pain as tears streaked his face.

"It's true!" he yelled as the poker crackled against his flesh.

The jailer held it there until the blood and sweat cooled the iron enough to no longer burn his skin. Korrith slipped into unconsciousness.

Korrith awoke with a sudden start, as if he were drowning. Water pooled at his feet, and the smell of wet earth mixed with the stench of burning meat. He was still bound to the heavy wooden chair.

The jailer set the pail down and glanced at the cleric, as if waiting for the next question.

"Korrith, absolve yourself in the eyes of Gate'har. Tell us the truth, magi, and this will go a lot easier," the cleric said with a heavy sigh.

"I-I-I am a mage, wh-who's only... crime was... being born different than you," Korrith stammered.

The cleric snorted. "You are an abomination of the magical arts. You and your kind bring death and destruction to our city, and expect leniency?" The cleric spat at him, the warm glob of saliva trailing down Korrith's bare skin.

Korrith said nothing, only glared at the cleric with contempt, knowing his fate had been sealed.

"Take him back to his cell. We'll continue this tomorrow," the cleric said, waving a dismissive hand at Korrith.

The jailer worked the leather straps loose and cuffed the heavy iron manacles back on Korrith's wrists. He pulled the mage to his feet and dragged him back to the cell. The heavy door slammed shut once he had been chained to the wall, leaving Korrith in the damp darkness of the jail. He was left alone with his thoughts of betrayal, loss, and dread.

Chapter 13

FALLING SPARK

"Y ou're lucky, magi. There's a crowd waitin' for ya up top," the jailer said as he slid the bolt back and opened the door.

Korrith moaned as he tried to move. His entire body was racked from the torture caused by the constant stream of questions he had no real answers for. Blood marked fresh wounds, while scabbed over and puss-filled pits marked older ones. His skin was pale and sickly. His clothes were all but shredded and offered him only the barest of modesty. His long hair and unkempt beard festered with lice.

"Come on, we mustn't keep them waiting," the jailer said as he unlocked his chain and pulled Korrith to his feet. He stumbled and fell.

The jailer growled, flung his arm underneath Korrith's, and dragged him to his feet.

"I do have to hand it to you, magi. I've never seen anyone last as long as you did," the jailer snickered as they walked out to the stone hallway.

Korrith didn't say anything. He had nothing to say. He had lost hope, had lost all sense of commonality with his fellow man. He was angry, resentful with the jailer and the clerics. He showed him his spite by spitting on the jailer's boot.

"Now, by gods. Why did you do that?" the jailer growled as he pushed Korrith in the small of his back, causing him to stumble into the wall. His head hit the smooth stone surface with a sickening crack, causing stars to explode across his vision.

"Another outburst like that, and I'll see to it personally you're not able to spit again."

Korrith was led up and out to the bright courtyard of the castle. The sun was high overhead, sending fangs of pure light into his eyes, blinding him.

"Move, you filthy magi," the jailer said, dragging him to the gallows.

There was a loud and boisterous crowd gathered around the front gate of the castle. Men and women of all walks of life cheered or booed his presence as he walked along the high stage of the gallows. A cleric watched from the other side.

Korrith was pushed up the steps, where a man and woman were waiting, nooses around their necks. He recognized the woman as the neighbor that had been dragged from her home. *How long ago had that been,* he wondered. She appeared haggard and defeated. Blood seeped down her legs and mouth.

Korrith's anger grew. *The monsters,* he thought. He felt his heart pounding in his chest, echoing in his ears.

The jailer fitted a noose around his neck and drew it tight. The hemp rope was coarse, pinching his skin as if rough hands were gripping his throat and squeezing. The smell of the city faded away, all his senses narrowed until all that remained was the sound of his breathing and his racing heart.

Korrith couldn't feel relief at being sent from this life. He was full of fury and spite. He hated them all. The mocking jeers, the lies they told themselves, the false safety they felt in his execution.

"By the power of Gate'har, I sentence these mages to death by hanging," the cleric said, causing the crowd to cheer in exultation.

Korrith's chest burned as he tried to hold his breath in. His heart thundered deafeningly in his ears.

The jailer walked over to the lever that controlled the false floor and yanked it hard.

Korrith felt the floor give. His last thought as his neck snapped was of Sorrna.

"The crowd, it sickens me," a mage whispered. "The only thing we have done was be born different."

"I heard there was talk of a rebellion," the other man sneered back.

"These arrogant men that place themselves as the judicators of mages, they are the abominations," the mage said quietly as he watched the bodies dangle in the gallows.

A bearded, well-built man with amber eyes and brown hair stepped between them, fixing the mage with a vile gaze. "I hear you're interested in starting a war. Perhaps my employer and I can assist you," he said with a wide, empty smile.

Voyage
of
Tears

Chapter 1

BY KINGS AND SOLDIERS

<hr>

C AIN SWUNG WIDE, MISSING his target.

The warrior he faced was a brute of a man. His square, statuesque features were set in a focused scowl. His grey-blue eyes were narrowed and fixed on him with a terrifying glare.

"You're slow, Cain. Come on, hit me!" the man spat.

Cain could taste blood, metallic and thick in his mouth. He had bit his lip from concentration and frustration. His bright, azure eyes narrowed at his opponent. The smell of damp earth hung heavy in the air around them.

The ax blade passed by. Cain felt the disrupted air brush his skin. "By the gods, Goa, we're just sparring!" Cain barely stood at Goa's shoulders, and what he lacked in muscle, he made up for in agility. His short-cropped, raven black hair glistened with moisture from sweat.

"Bah, do you think your enemies will be so forgiving?" Goa asked with a hearty laugh. He hefted the ax up then swung it in an arc.

Cain rolled away just to keep from being decapitated. *Goa was not playing,* he thought as sweat trickled down his face.

Goa managed to bring his weapon back in front of him as Cain stood.

"Wait, what are—" With a mighty downward swing, Goa buried his ax between Cain's feet, missing them by inches. Cain swallowed hard; he wasn't prepared for that. Sweat stung his eyes, blurring them momentarily.

Goa glared at him. "You get distracted too easily. If I wanted to, I could have killed you right then."

The clouds above them hung low and dark, threatening to dump warm spring rain on the military compound and surrounding city. The two men stared at one another, adjusting their footing as the other moved in the packed dirt and gravel. The sound of swords clashing faded into background noise, their focus intent on one another.

"That's enough, you two," a commanding voice boomed. "Line up." Commander Zell's sharp eyes glared at them. Scars from years of military service crisscrossed his thick, tan skin. Greying hair swayed in a topknot as he walked toward them with authority.

"Yes, sir!" the men said in unison as they rushed to set weapons and shields down on the racks next to the sparring field. They snapped into line with several other soldiers along the combat ring. The Sword of Justice Compound was large, taking up a portion of the ground between the Gate'har citadel to their west and the Xonthian Navel yard to their east.

"I've been given orders to select a team of men. While I cannot yet tell you what that mission is, I can tell you it will be treacherous," Zell said. Cain and the rest of his unit stood at attention, their eyes forward, their bodies motionless in front of the commander. Cain felt a shiver of anticipation crawl up his spine.

"It was my intention to select a handful of you for this mission, but in light of its political implications, we are not afforded that luxury."

Cain's eyes widened at the idea he might be selected for a mission. He licked his lips and glanced at Zell expectantly.

"Instead, I have decided this entire squad will be dispatched. You leave in two days; get your affairs in order and form up at the King's Dock one hour before sunrise two days from now, for briefing. Dismissed!"

Cain looked over his shoulder at Goa, who was grinning mischievously. "Are they shipping us off to some exotic locale?" Goa asked, eyes twinkling.

Cain turned and clapped his friend on the shoulder. "I doubt they'd be sending you. If they sent just me? Sure, of course, it'd be some place divine. The fact they're sending us all? I don't think so. It'll be hell."

"It could happen," Goa said as his excitement melted away to a frown. "You're such a killer of joy."

Cain shook his head and laughed. "Come on, I'll buy the first round."

Port Orlynns was a major shipping hub for Xonthian, where the majority of the kingdom's navy was stationed. Large oak and pine trees dotted the city. Its crooked, hard-packed roads were alive with the movement of horses, carts, and residents as they went about their lives.

Between the residential, military, and warehouse districts was situated The Broken Wheel, a well-worn tavern partially obscured by the encroaching wilderness. It was popular with the travelers and sailors that traversed between the two areas.

The Broken Wheel smelled old. Lichen and other creeping greenery clung to the wooded exterior. Boards had splintered, and some had broken off, sitting in the mud around it. Trees scraped the shingled roof, as if knocking politely in a vain attempt at entry. Despite this, however, it was clean and welcoming. Controlled chaos swirled around the common room as the sometimes rowdy guests boasted about their conquests. Patrons of all kinds—merchants, soldiers, and even locals—frequented the large pub. A fireplace sat dark and cold in the corner, while the normally closed smoke-stained windows stood open, letting air from the outside mix with the odors of the tavern.

Cain and Goa sat at a bench-style table with several other soldiers from their unit on their left, while a few merchants sat on their right. The beer-stained wood felt smooth from decades of wear. The waitress was tasked with keeping the ale flowing, dodging and dancing in and out of guests' reach, expertly taking orders and delivering fresh mugs.

Cain watched her and chuckled. Soldiers and merchants tried grabbing hold of her to no avail. Her agility and years of experience kept her moving, while a smile and a wink kept the men happy. It was the married men, however, Cain felt more akin to. They were polite and didn't spend time doting on the young blonde barmaid as she came by.

"She must make a killing in tips here," Goa said with a low whistle.

Cain snapped his attention back toward him. "Huh? Oh. Yeah, probably."

"Think I stand a chance?" Goa asked, running a hand through his hair.

"No."

Goa looked at him dejectedly.

Cain smiled and took a drink from his whisky. The smooth, woody liquid burned as he swallowed it.

"Whatever," Goa muttered as he drank deeply from his stein.

Cain chuckled. "So, where do you think we'll be deployed?"

"Ugh." Goa set his mug down with a loud thunk. "Like you pointed out, nowhere good, I'm sure. The fact that we're being shipped out means overseas somewhere."

"I bet it's got something to do with the filthy magi," a voice from their left interrupted. Morik, another of the men in Cain's unit, was a short, stubby man with thick brown hair and bushy eyebrows. He looked almost like a dwarf if it wasn't for his unusually smooth and hairless skin. Pearly black eyes peered at Cain, glossy from the heavy drinking.

"What do you mean?" Goa asked, brows furrowed.

Morik drew closer. The stench of his body, a pungent onion smell, was only barely covered by the odor of alcohol coming from his breath. "Haven't you noticed all the prisoner wagons coming into town?"

Cain shook his head and shrugged as he glanced at Goa, who also looked perplexed.

"It's true, they've been arriving in droves lately," Morik slurred.

"Ze king has signed a new decree," a man on their other side said as he leaned in. "I'm sorry, I overheard Ze conversation. My name is Wi'ir der'Handler. At your service." He bowed his head in polite greeting.

"Well met. I'm Cain, this is Goa and Morik. Pleasure," Cain said, studying the man. His accent was that of a local. He looked as though he could have given Goa a rough time if he were inclined to violence, but his vibrant, neatly pressed attire told another story. He was dressed like a merchant—one that had done well for himself. He made the soldiers in the tavern look like street urchins in comparison.

"What do you mean?" Cain asked, looking between Morik and Wi'ir.

"Don't look at me, I didn't know anything about that," Morik said, holding his hands up as he sat back.

"His Majesty announced a few days ago zat he vas putting a stop to executions vhere zere vas no murder. Simply existing as a mage no longer elicits a death penalty," Wi'ir explained.

"That should please the bleeding-heart sympathizers," Goa muttered.

"Tensions have been high for several months from both sides. Why the change?" Cain asked.

"Magic users don't see ze harm in zeir magic; some even vurk for ze kingdoms. People vere beginning to question ze hypocrisy in zat. And..." Wi'ir trailed off, then looked around conspiratorially before continuing. "Ze Clerics of Gate'har. Zey vere overreaching."

"That I believe. They've become zealots lately. But I can see the hypocrisy, though; the clerics, too, cast magic. Why are they allowed to?" Cain asked with a shake of his head.

"You... Don't get soft on me now!" Goa said loudly, slapping the table in emphasis.

"Zat vas ze question ze King began to ask. Zere had been a large summit on zat vary topic. His majesty did not like vhat ze clerics had said apparently, and so, a new declaration," Wi'ir said as he sat back and took a swing from a wine glass. "In any case, it is late and I must be off."

Goa and Cain nodded to the merchant, who stood and bowed his farewell before pushing his way through the crowd to the door.

Morik leaned forward again, causing Goa and Cain to look at him expectantly. "You don't think we'll be escorting the filthy mages to their new home, do you?"

Cain looked at Goa. Both said, "No," simultaneously, before erupting in laughter.

Chapter 2

BROKEN HEARTS

WATER POURED FROM THE black sky. Lightning shattered the darkness, illuminating the city in bright yellow and blue light with manic frequency. People hurried through the rain, busy with their nightly tasks or returning home after a long day of work. Cain was in no hurry and sloshed nonchalantly toward the apartment he shared with his girlfriend, which she had bought shortly after they met.

It had been hot and humid for several days, and the cleansing, cool water washed away the stress of training and drills. Cain lifted his face to the deluge, the rain pouring over his features.

Her bright, youthful face appeared in front of him and he smiled. She was short, with dark brown hair with a tinge of red. Her dark blue eyes were exotic and drew him in, like the shadows of deep sleep. It had been a few days since he had seen Korra, and if it wasn't for the deployment, he would still be sleeping in the barracks.

A shiver ran up his spine thinking of the last time they were together. He was thankful for the cool rain as he felt his skin flush red hot at the images. He couldn't wait to rekindle that tonight.

His heavy, wet footfalls were replaced by loud echoes as he entered the stone alleyway of the apartment complex. It emptied into a rounded courtyard, with several stairs that went up to the second-floor rooms.

Warm light from a small window welcomed him and gave him the knowledge Korra was still awake. He took the key from his pocket and fumbled with the lock until the door opened and granted him passage inside.

The large, single room apartment smelled of spices—she must have baked recently— and his mouth watered from the imagined tastes. The bed was off-center against the far wall and his eyes were fixed on its occupants.

He stared, mouth agape. His mind tried to make sense of the scene, and for a split second, he thought he had stumbled into the wrong apartment.

"Cain!" Korra gasped as she jerked the blankets up to cover her naked breasts. His vision constricted as her voice confirmed he had the right place, and a fire of rage ignited in his breast.

The man next to her stumbled out from under the covers and landed on the floor naked. He fumbled through the pile of clothes around the bed and finding his pants, pulled them on.

Cain watched, detached, a myriad of thoughts, feelings, and desires racing through his mind. He saw himself beating the man senseless. His chest ached as if his heart was trying to claw its way out, intent on murder. He fought the torrent of emotions and stared dumbfounded. By the looks of the lanky man, he was a commoner, someone that would go unnoticed in the streets. An unkept mop of brown hair sat atop his narrow head. Cain settled on anger and clenched his fist along with his jaw as time narrowed to a single point and slowed down.

"Please, Cain," Korra pleaded.

His hand gripped the dagger at his belt, his knuckles white from the strain. He slid it from the sheath and stalked toward the man. Terror filled in the man's eyes. Cain bent down and picked up a discarded shirt; it was red and would work perfectly.

"Wait— Wha—" the man stammered.

Cain leveled the dagger at him and fixed him with a glare; every fiber of his being was fighting the urge to plunge the blade through his heart. The man threw his hands up in surrender and backed away.

Cain turned his attention slowly back to Korra, who was crying in the bed, the sheets pulled to her neck. He slid the dagger into the shirt and cut a swath of cloth. His eyes never leaving hers as they reflected the pain and anger at her. He took the cloth and walked to the door of the apartment. With a loud thunk, he buried the dagger into the wood frame of the door, the tattered clothing hanging like a flag. With a clenched fist, he hammered on the hilt of the dagger, fixing it in place. With a glare, he growled, "Now everyone will know there's a whore living here."

Cain stalked out the door, his cheeks flush with contained rage and hurt. His clenched fist, numb from the strain.

Cain wanted to slam the door to the barracks shut as he entered, but decided that wouldn't help him right now. He walked over to his bunk and sat down. His jaw hurt from clenching his teeth, and his clothes were soaked through, sending cold shivers through his body. He slumped back onto the bed in defeat.

"What happened?" Goa asked in a whisper from the top bunk as he looked over the side at Cain.

Cain stared up at the bottom of the bunk above him, his lips pursed. His eyes burned with repressed emotions.

"Damn," Goa said quietly. "Did Korra...?"

Cain turned over on his side, away from Goa peering down at him. Leaving his friend to wonder what to say or do next. The bed shifted as Goa lay back down in silence.

Chapter 3

<hr>

HMS HORNIRITH

THE RAIN HAD STOPPED, leaving behind the heavy grey clouds in the sky. The pre-dawn light was muted and darker than it typically would be without the overcast weather. *It reflects my mood, I suppose,* Cain thought as he stood at the entrance of the dock with the rest of the men, waiting for Commander Zell.

The King's Dock pier took up a swath of beach between the naval station and the Swords of Justice base. Several vessels bobbed alongside the large wooden piers that stretched out into Halfmoon Bay.

"Line up!" a voice boomed, cutting through the idle chatter of the gathered men, demanding their attention.

Cain was already in position when the rest of the men snapped to attention next to him. But it wasn't Commander Zell that had called for them to fall in.

"Coattes," Cain growled under his breath.

The soldier was arrogant, loud, and angry. He was the same size as Cain, but heavier in girth with round features that hid his muscle. Narrow blue eyes judged everyone he surveyed, as if weighing their worth. Thin black hair covered his head and forearms, and he had an unshaven and grungy face.

"Get in line, Coattes," Commander Zell said as he walked toward the dock. He led a procession of plainly armored city guards, who were dragging bound men and women between them.

Shit, he thought. *That merchant in the bar was right.*

"As you can surmise, you will be escorting these mages to a new home. As some of you may have heard, his majesty has declared all mages not sanctioned by the Kingdom of Xonthian or Cettera as outlaws. As such, anyone found practicing magic unlawfully will be sentenced to exile," Commander Zell said as he nodded to the closest city guard. The man yanked on the chain locked to the shackles of a mage, causing him to stumble up the gangway toward the ship.

Cain watched from the corner of his eye as they were led up. Most were plain-looking men and women of various sizes, ages, and demeanor. The one that caught his attention, however, was a fiery red-headed woman with sharp grey eyes that glared at them as she passed. Her slender body held none of the shame the rest of the chained-up mages had.

"You eight men will oversee their journey to the Fire Isles," the commander said, snapping Cain's attention back to Zell. "Your orders are to keep them locked up, and ensure no harm comes to them or yourselves."

"Yes, sir!" the men said.

"Stow your gear and assist the sailors in launching. This isn't a pleasure cruise; you'll have your assignments once on board. Dismissed!" Commander Zell commanded with a salute.

The unit returned the salute and filtered their way onboard. The mages were led below deck using the ladder leading to the forward hold. Cain looked down the stairs to the main cabin area below the deck. He followed Goa down the steep wood planks to the main area, where the men would be sleeping. Hammocks hung along each side of the ship's hull, with a column taking up the center of the room.

"Ugh, filthy magi scum," Coattes spat as he pushed his way past Cain and Goa into the sleeping quarters.

"Are we being punished?" Morik said as he followed on the heels of Coattes.

The other men filtered into the room and selected their hammock. There were already a few occupied by bags. It had to be the crew. This wasn't a cruise; there were no passengers.

Coattes walked over to one, near the porthole, and tossed the previous occupant's gear on the floor near the pillar.

Cain stowed his gear in a chest under his hammock and turned to Goa, who took the bunk above him. "I'm not in any mood for..." He trailed off and looked over his shoulder. Goa followed his gaze and nodded.

"This is going to be a rough voyage," Goa sighed.

"Line up on deck!" a voice called down the stairs in a thick, rough commanding echo.

The soldiers clambered up the steps to the main deck of the ship and stood at attention. Since they were on a ship, the men wore simple leather armor with the emblem of the Sword of Justice stamped into the center plate. It allowed them protection but also kept their movement free. The change from their heavier chain and plate armor felt freeing.

Cain had expected to see seamen from the Xonthian Navy aboard the ship; however, the sailors lined up behind them were clothed in plain, tattered rags and worn shirts that had been over mended. They lacked the distinct uniforms of grey-blue.

Heavy boots thudded from the helm as the captain appeared at the rail to look down at the men gathered below. Cain was jolted by the appearance of the well-dressed merchant he had met at the tavern the previous night.

"Good morning, I am Captain Wi'ir der'Handler. You are standing on my ship, ze Hornirith. Vhile you are on my ship, you vill do as I instruct. Is zat clear?"

Cain shot Goa a shocked, wide-eyed glance before yelling his affirmation with the rest of the men.

"Now, my first mate, Zachis here, has your duties. It vill be posted below vhen he's done reading it. Zere are no exceptions, and I vill not accept failure. I run a clean ship for his Majesty, and being as you are eizer Swords of Justice or my usual hand-picked crew, I expect everyone to be on zeir best behavior," Wi'ir said as he motioned for the man standing next to him to step forward.

Zachis was shorter than Wi'ir. Muscular, hairless arms held a piece of parchment. His narrow-face looked weathered from decades of seafaring. His piercing amber eyes surveyed the crew appraisingly before listing everyone's duties. Cain shared guard duty with Coattes, Goa, and Morik, while the rest of their unit helped the sailors. Zachis climbed down the steps and nailed the list to the door frame leading to the galley.

Cain let out long sigh; guard duty was the better end of the short stick. He did not want to spend his time cleaning and repairing the ship. That did not sound like fun.

"You have your assignments," Wi'ir said, stepping to the rail. "Cast off. Unfurl ze mainsail and stow ze cords. Pull in ze lines. Move!"

Chapter 4

GUILTY OF HATE

THEY SAILED FROM HALFMOON Bay, leaving the safety of the harbor for the open sea and the long voyage that lay before them. The unmarked, white sails stretched along the thick wood beams, causing the ship to creak against the strain of wind and water. Cain, along with most of the Swords of Justice soldiers, helped the deckhands prepare the ship. By late afternoon, most of the work and chores had been completed. The smell of the saltwater became pure and fresh, unlike the stale and decaying fish stench the harbor smelled of. The setting sun turned the clean air chilly.

"I can't believe her, you know?" Goa sat down beside Cain on the bench in the cramped galley, where the men were being served dinner. Morik and a handful of sailors who introduced themselves as Fest, Borris, Mika, and Lorre ate ravenously. They were stringy men with rough hands, thick skin, and sunken eyes that had seen their share of hard times on the high seas.

Cain nodded as he shoved a piece of bread in his mouth. "Me either."

"You're a better man than me; I would have punched the man's lights out," Goa said, slamming his fist on the table, causing the bowls and plates to dance angrily. The men around them glared at him.

Cain chewed, then swallowed before responding. "The thought had occurred to me."

"I guess it's luck we're out here then, more time for you to decide what to do next," Goa said with a smile. "Maybe return to Xonthian City?"

"This is an easy dispatch; why would you want to give this up for the city?" Morik asked nosily.

"No, I think I'll stay in Port Orlynns. The place has grown on me," Cain replied, before taking another bite of dinner and ignoring the eavesdropping Morik.

"Good, I didn't want to have to go either," Goa chuckled. "I'd be lost without my sparring partner!"

Cain rolled his eyes and finished his drink. "Morik, isn't it about time for you to relieve Coattes?"

"Eh, yes. I figured he wouldn't mind a few more minutes with the magi scum. I'm sure he's having a good time down—"

"Morik, you bastard! Get down here!" Coattes's voice cut through the thick teak wood walls of the ship.

"I don't think he's having fun," Cain chuckled.

Morik sighed and stood, finishing his drink as he did. The stout soldier shuffled his way from the galley toward the ladder leading to the brig.

Cain watched him disappear before turning to Goa. "I should have hit him."

"Morik?"

"No, the asshole who stole my girl," Cain replied irritably.

Goa chuckled. "Might have made you feel better."

"Would it?"

"You would have likely ended up in the brig yourself," Goa said with a shrug.

Cain sighed. "Yeah."

"Don't let it get you down. There are plenty of fish in the sea," Goa said with a wave of his hand, motioning to the vast ocean outside.

Coattes stalked into the galley, where he picked a plate of food up and sat down angrily at the cramped table. Cain and Goa watched as he ate frantically, huddled over the plate as if someone would steal it, a look of contempt on his gruff face.

Fest stood and left, unable to weather the storm of spite rolling off the angry soldier. The remaining sailors watched him cautiously but talked quietly among themselves.

"Filthy magi, make me sick," Coattes said as he tore a piece of bread viciously apart.

"You seem to be taking their presence personally," Goa said evenly. "They kick your puppy when you were a kid or something?"

Coattes slowly turned his gaze to Goa and stared coldly. Cain clenched his fists instinctively, ready for a fight.

"You remember when that mage burned down half the slums in Xonthian City?" Coattes asked with a low growl. "I was there."

"You were there when it happened?" Cain asked, somewhat skeptically.

"I was stationed there, yes," Coattes said as he turned back to his plate of food.

"Did the mage kill someone you know?"

"No."

"Then why such animosity?"

Coattes threw his bread down and whirled toward Cain, his eyes glaring with fury. "They are unnatural to the gods' will! They do not deserve to sully the sacred earth we live upon."

Goa put a hand on Coattes shoulder in anticipation of the man leaping over the table to attack Cain.

Coattes looked down at the hand and then it's owner with a glower. "Remove it, before I remove it for you."

"You're a powder keg on a boat full of sparks," Goa warned him with a glare, before setting his arm back down on the table. "Watch it, or you may end up taking us all with you."

Coattes stood quickly and spat on the floor, his eyes burrowing into Goa. He turned and stomped toward the main deck.

Cain and Goa watched him leave, then shook their heads collectively in dismay. They stood and cleared their plates before heading to the bunk room below deck. The shifting ship lulled them into sleep.

Chapter 5

GUARDS OF JUSTICE

Cain jolted upright, tangling himself in the hammock above him. He cursed his clumsiness. The nightmare he had faded from memory, overwritten with the frustration and embarrassment of being startled awake.

Having slept in his armor, all he had to do was pull on his boots when he climbed out of the hammock, before stumbling his way to the brig. Morik nodded at him and stood from the chair he had tipped back against the wall. "Mornin'," he said stifling a yawn.

Cain nodded as Morik stood and stretched. "Anything exciting?"

"No, they've been quiet," Morik replied.

"Alright. Have a good nap then," Cain said as he leaned against the wall.

Morik waved sleepily and disappeared upstairs, leaving Cain to watch over the prisoners. The cage itself was as wide as the ship and nearly the same size deep. The bars were oddly colored, specially designed by the clerics to keep magic from being used. Their black and silver surfaces glistened with moisture from the salty sea air. The stench of unwashed bodies and full chamber pots hung heavily in the brig.

He sat down on the chair Morik had occupied and leaned back. His eyes scanned the occupants of the prison; they were a mix of men and women from all corners of Xonthian. From the darker-skinned oasis dwellers of Yenzu, to the golden-haired North Kelsa plainsmen. Then there was the red-head, who sat in the corner, her knees pulled to her chest. She was a mystery. He couldn't put a finger on where she was from. Her fair skin indicated she may be from Xonthian City, but her narrow, grey eyes, almost almond shape in appearance, were something else. And she was glaring at him.

Cain quickly looked away, realizing she had noticed his probing gaze.

"We're not some sideshow freaks, you know. We're human just like you." Her thin voice had an edge so sharp it might have cut him, if he were any closer.

"I-I'm sorry," Cain replied.

"You Swords of Justice are all the same—impassionate, soulless killers," she spat.

Cain shifted in his chair.

"Shhh, Lillia, you'll make him mad," an older mage said. He comforted her with a frail hand on her shoulder. Lillia waved a dismissive hand and stood. Her gown was torn and stained with unrecognizable filth. She walked to edge of the cell and stared at the bars. She raised her hands to them, hovering her palms just over their black and silver surface as if testing it, unsure if they would zap her. She tentatively grasped them before glaring through to Cain. The rest of the mages collectively sighed, as if they, too, were relieved they were not in danger by accidently touching the bars.

"I'm sorry, I didn't mean to—"

"Sorry for what? Persecuting us? Exiling us? Treating us like animals?" Lillia asked.

"No, I—"

"No, of course you wouldn't. You're a zealot, like the rest of your kind." She spat at Cain's feet.

Cain stared at her in dismay, his brows furrowed. He opened his mouth to speak but shut it again. There was nothing he could say. She wasn't wrong.

She slid down the bars to sit and drew her knees up to her chin once again, her eyes never leaving his.

Cain watched her openly now; he felt sorry for her—for them. So, he took a chance and asked a question that would likely anger them. "Why are you here?" he inquired slowly, before swallowing hard.

Lillia laughed hollowly. "Our 'king' betrayed us."

"No, I mean, what did you do to deserve being here?"

Lillia jumped to her feet in anger, her hands clenched in fists. "We did NOTHING! We were simply born!"

"That's not what I meant. What did you do, magic wise, that brought you here?" Cain asked.

Lillia looked taken aback for a split second before recovering her anger. She walked to the bars again and stared at him. Cain was thankful for the barrier between them. "I was living my life, at home, with my husband and two children, when a neighbor saw me using a spell to start a fire. The next thing I know, my husband is dead on the ground and my children are being dragged away by the Gate'har Paladins."

Cain looked at her, his mouth slightly agape at both her words and the ferocity in them. Aside from that, however, he had no reply. There was no comfort he could give. He couldn't imagine the kind of loss, pain, anger, and hatred she had. A pang of guilt fluttered through his stomach.

"Nothing? You going to just stare at me now? I told you my story and now you can't even speak?" Lillia snorted and shook her head. "At least your comrades didn't ask questions."

"Thank you," Cain said finally. He regained his composure and leaned forward before rubbing his face. He looked up at her. "I did ask, and I wanted to know. Thank you for sharing."

It was Lillia's turn to study him, a look of confusion playing briefly across her dirt-covered features. They sat in silence for several moments. She watched with guarded eyes, while Cain stared at the floor, feeling the weight of her gaze.

After what seemed like an eternity, she returned to her spot in the cell and sat down heavily.

Cain sat back in the chair and folded his arms in front of him, taking a deep, steady breath. He watched her, studied her every line, every crease in her face, every curl on her head, and the way the folds of her clothes fell over her body. Cain let the breath out slowly in a long sigh, as if he was being deflated.

They sat in relative silence, listening to the waves gently lapping across the hull. Minutes ticked to hours as time flew by like the water outside.

Goa stomped down the stairs with a tray in his hand. Lunch had been served. Leftovers had been combined with a few new ingredients to make a stew of meat and vegetables beside a slice of bread. The smell of broth was warm and comforting. Goa served Cain his share before handing the remaining bowls to the prisoners.

"They behaving themselves?" he asked as he regarded Cain with a stern look.

"Yes," he replied as he took a bite of food. "Thanks for the meal."

"Bah, it was either that or Morik would eat it all."

Cain laughed, although there was no mirth behind it.

"Well, I got this. Go on, enjoy the sun for a bit," Goa said, handing him the tray. "I'll collect the bowls when they're done. You can get them when ya bring me dinner."

Cain stood with a nod and took the tray under his arm. He glanced back over his shoulder discreetly and looked at Lillia once more before ascending the stairs. *I'll find a way to talk with her again,* he promised himself.

Chapter 6

CONVERSATIONS WITH A MAGE

L IFE ABOARD THE HMS Hornirith rushed by as the ship cut through the water like a spear through flesh and blood. The sound of waves brushing against the bow of the ship turned to white noise, lulling Cain to sleep. When he awoke the next morning for his shift, he dressed and quietly made his way to the brig.

"Morning," Morik said. He stretched, setting the chair back down that had been propped against the wall, as if he had been sitting reclined.

"Good morning, Morik. Anything new?" Cain asked conversationally as the soldier stood and started toward the stairs.

"No, they've been quiet. Mostly sleeping."

Cain nodded and watched as Morik disappeared upstairs. Cain surveyed the mages through the cage bars and saw most of them were still asleep. A few were huddled together for companionship and warmth, while some sat against the bars with their heads bowed in slumber. Lillia was in the corner, curled up in a ball.

Cain sat down and watched her. Her small frame rose and fell in a slow, steady rhythm. A wry smile pulled at the side of his mouth. He shook his head and sat back with a sigh. *Ugh, what am I doing? Haven't I had enough trouble with women as of late?* he scolded himself, then chuckled. *Fool.*

He gazed back and saw she was stirring awake. She stretched like a feline awaking from a pleasant night's sleep before rolling into a sitting position, her legs crisscrossed. She glanced up at him with a blank expression. Her eyes were dull and restless.

"What?" she asked.

"Excuse me?"

"What are you looking at?"

Cain shrugged. "I meant no offense; I was just making sure everyone was healthy."

She laughed hollowly, causing some of the remaining mages to awake with a start. "What do you care?"

"I suppose I don't," he replied.

She watched him for a minute, then stood and walked to the bars. "Then why?"

Shit, now what do I say? He peered around as if looking for someone to jump in, but there was no one. "We're still a long way from the Fire Isles; I wanted to make sure we didn't have any deaths this early in our voyage."

She snickered in reply.

His mind slowed at her response. *She bought it,* he thought. What was he doing? He was acting like a child with a crush. He wrung his hands together but stopped abruptly for fear of being seen.

"You don't want us to die because it'd make you look bad," she said with a wry smile. "Rich, I suppose, coming from someone like you."

Cain raised a quizzical brow at her. "I'm sorry?"

"You've had everything handed to you. You probably come from a well-off family in Xonthian City," Lillia said, her grey eyes probing his gaze as if trying to read his mind. "So, what do you care if a few magi scum croak in the night? You'd sooner toss us overboard than shed a tear."

"Well, there's a report I'd have to write and—"

She laughed, and for the first time, he saw mirth soften her expression. It was intoxicating.

"It's true," he replied indignantly.

Her features quickly hardened, returning her to the stoic countenance that years of loss and anger had grown around her.

"But," he began, "you're right. I am from a well-off family in Xonthian City. I left there when I was young to join the Swords of Justice. I wanted nothing to do with them, though. My family, I mean."

"Because you wanted to impose your will over helpless men, women, and children, like me?" she asked coldly.

He sighed and shook his head. "No. In fact, the civil unrest between mages and... everyone else hadn't yet sparked into the flames it is today."

She watched him but said nothing until, finally, he continued. "The clerics of Gate'har don't command the Swords of Justice, the King does," he said, glancing up at her.

"And here you are, under orders to take us to an island home, where we'll surely die a slow and painful death," she said bitterly.

"I can't speak for the king. From my perspective, I have no quarrel with you or any mage," he said slowly, unsure if he should be saying anything at all.

"You lie," she growled. "All men without our gift look down upon us. Like we're some sort of freak of nature."

"No, that's a lie you tell yourself at night to let you sleep," Cain said, looking at her. A lump in his chest had grown, either from fear or anger he couldn't tell.

She stared at him for a moment, unsure how to respond. He could tell she had overplayed her hand.

"You are correct about one thing though," he said after several seconds of uneasy silence. "I am under orders. But what you fail to realize, however, is that we're to bring you safely to your new home on the Fire Isles. That is the king's decree. So, to answer your question earlier, I don't want anyone to die on my watch because having someone pass on this voyage would be going against his majesty's orders."

Anger flared in her grey eyes, and he could tell she wanted to shout at him, but she had no words.

Cain sighed and stood; dragging the chair closer but just out of reach of the bars, he sat back down and leaned forward. "I don't want to fight. Why... Why don't you tell me about your children?"

Lillia's eyes flew open wide before she could control them. Her stony expression softened slightly as if the wall around her crumbled.

"It's alright, you don't have to tell me," he said, suddenly feeling guilty for having asked.

She dropped her gaze down at her feet, then back up at him through the bars. "Mia and Den. They were my everything."

Cain looked at her and smiled gently but said nothing, giving her time to continue.

"Six and eight. Mia was the youngest; she was full of life. Den was like me, though, full of..." She trailed off and peered up at Cain, her eyes glossy. "No. You don't deserve to hear about their lives."

Cain watched as the softened wall around her rebuilt itself. Her eyes grew stormy, and he could feel the spite and anger slither around them as if she was pulling it all in for material.

"Why won't you leave me be? Do you hate us so much that you enjoy torturing us?"

"No, that's not it, I—" He stopped, mouth agape. He didn't have an explanation.

"You what?" she asked, narrowing her eyes.

"I'm sorry, I didn't mean to offend you. I genuinely wanted to know."

She stood and glared down at him. "You don't deserve an explanation."

Cain watched as she walked to the farthest corner from him and sat down. Drawing her knees up, she wrapped her arms around them. He pulled the chair away from the cage and sat back down, a pang of guilt settling in his stomach.

The rest of the day went by uneventfully and melted into the next. The air of uneasiness thickened, leaving Cain guilty and anxious. It poisoned his thoughts like a festering wound. Finally, after he couldn't stand the silence any further, he walked over to the bars, looming over her.

"Look, I'm sorry. I don't know what else I can say. I-I..." He let out a long sigh as his words abandoned him, and his shoulders slowly slumped. "My brother. Edger. He was a mage."

Her gaze fluttered up at him guardedly, but she said nothing.

Cain kneeled on his haunches and continued. "I was probably nine, or ten maybe, when the clerics of Gate'har began to come around. They were worried about his power. He could control earth, and they were very much interested in him joining the Gate'har clerics."

"He was twelve at the time. I was jealous of him. I wanted magical powers as well. I would go outside and try hard to get the pebbles to move, water, anything, but it never happened. One day, he came outside and saw me. He sat down, and I remember him smiling at me. He told me I was better than he was for not having the powers he did, that I was destined to become someone greater. I wasn't tethered to the responsibility it came with.

"I didn't understand it then. When we were older, I wanted to join the Swords of Justice, so I did. He, however, couldn't find a job. No one wanted a mage working for them by then; the world had started to grow jealous, as I had been. The world didn't have someone like my brother shaping their lives and molding them into something better. I didn't know it then, but when my brother was killed, murdered by a mob of zealous protestors, he was right. He was tethered to responsibilities I didn't fully comprehend. So, no, I don't hate you or your kind, and I'm sorry we're here at this point."

Cain stood and walked back to the chair and sat, his limbs shaking from the restrained emotions. He never told anyone about his brother. Not even Goa knew. He rubbed his face and took a slow, steadying breath and pushed the past from his mind.

Chapter 7

THE FIGHT

CAIN STOOD AT THE entry to the galley. The bags under his eyes had grown larger and darker from the lack of sleep. The ship had tossed and turned more than he had, and it was grating on his nerves. He sighed and shuffled toward the bench in the center of the room and sat down at the table.

He was in a daze, frustrated at all the resurfacing emotions of losing his brother—the anger and the sadness. It all bubbled up and mixed with the betrayal from losing Korra. He rubbed his face as if trying to tear away the feelings.

The cook, a clean-pressed, lithe man, walked over and dropped a plate of food down in front of him. "Don't expect me to serve you every time, ya bum."

Cain chuckled. "Sorry, I'm still waking up."

"Aye, right," he said, and returned to his boiling pot of stew.

"What? No silverware?" Cain laughed and threw up his hands in jest as the cook whirled around with a murderous glare.

Cain stood and walked over to the serving table where the dishes were stored and collected a fork and a glass of water. As he turned back to the table, Borris and Mika, two of the sailors on duty, entered the galley. They collected food and sat down at the opposite end of the table.

"You sure you saw a ship?" Borris asked Mika.

Cain sat down at his plate and picked at his meal as he eavesdropped on the two sailors.

"I'm sure of it," Mika replied quietly.

"What'd Zachis say?" Borris asked.

"Nothin', only nodded and said he'd keep an eye on it."

"The ship may have been too far away to make sense of their purpose, or affiliation."

"Naw, I'm tellin' ya, it's following us, sure as the sun sets," Morik said before taking a bite of bread.

"Who'd want to steal from us? We ain't haulin' anything valuable," Borris said as he shook his head in dismay and took a bite from his stew.

Cain looked up from his meal in time to see Coattes darkening the doorway.

"Argh!" Coattes stormed into the galley, his anger cutting through the calm of the room. "If I have to spend any more time with those ungrateful magi, I'm going to vomit."

Cain sighed and ate faster as Coattes served himself then sat down in front of him.

"I tell you what, though, that red-headed magi, I bet she's a fire in bed," Coattes said as he shoveled food into his maw like a predator that had been starved.

"They are people, like anyone else," Cain mumbled under his breath.

Coattes stopped chewing and looked up at him. He laughed, spraying half-eaten food onto Cain's plate.

Cain's lip curled up in a snarl as he pushed the contaminated dish away, glaring across the table at Coattes, hoping he would disappear.

"Don't tell me you're sympathetic to those magi?" Coattes asked as he wiped his mouth with the back of a grimy hand.

Cain stood to leave, but Coattes's evil laugh stopped him. He turned and growled. "You're a disgrace to the Swords of Justice."

"So says the magi lover," Coattes snarled, pushing to his feet with a vehemence that made the dishes on the table rattle. He leaned forward, his narrowed gaze fixed on Cain. "I bet you have eyes for that red-head magi filth, don't you? You are always the lady's man."

Cain made for the door. Angered flare across his face, turning it red, although, he wasn't sure if it was from anger or embarrassment.

As he reached the door, Coattes laughed again. "Yeah, run off to your whore. Since I'm not worthy of this uniform, maybe I'll pay her a visit later myself."

Cain's vision blurred and he whirled at Coattes. A clenched fist struck out; the hair on Coattes's head fluttered as the strike sailed harmlessly past. The room erupted in activity as the men exchanged blows, crashing into chairs and landing on the table. The sailors stood and tried to break them up, while the cook yelled obscenities in an attempt to make them stop.

Coattes's elbow cracked across Cain's face, causing tears to well in his eyes, blurring his vision momentarily. Cain grabbed the man's neck and squeezed it with both hands. They rolled off the table and onto the floor. Coattes landed on top and punched Cain relentlessly.

Coattes swung wildly, nearly hitting the sailors as they grab him and pulled him off.

"Enough!" a commanding voice echoed through the room.

Cain stood, wiping blood from the corner of his mouth, murderous intent in his eyes.

The sailors held Coattes back as he returned the look, oblivious to the first mate's entry.

Zachis surveyed the two men, then pointed out toward the deck. "You two, outside, now!"

The sailors reluctantly let Coattes go. He stomped toward the main deck, Zachis and Cain close behind.

Once outside, they lined up at attention, anger still clearly visible on their features. Zachis walked over to them and glared, irritation etched across his face.

"As Wi'ir had said, we run a tight ship. Insubordination of this magnitude is NOT tolerated. Whatever the quarrel is between you two, it is insignificant on this vessel. If one of us fails in our duties, we all suffer," Zachis growled, his eyes darting between the two men. "Therefore, since you two have so much energy, you will clean the entire ship, from sail to stern, on top of your guard duties. If you complain, fall behind, or so much as glare in one another's direction, you will be tied to the mainmast and lashed. Do I make myself clear?"

"Yes, sir!" the two men replied.

"You will start by cleaning the galley and apologizing to the cook. Now, get out of my sight," Zachis spat.

"Yes, sir!" they said in unison, before turning and walking off toward the galley.

How could I let myself get lured so easily? Cain thought, his head bowed in shame. He sighed and followed Coattes into the galley. His anger subsided with each beat of his heart, as if the blood that had been fuel a moment ago was now cooling his emotions.

Chapter 8

◆

LOVE AND LIFE

"A H, THERE YOU ARE," Morik said. "Was beginning to wonder if you'd show up."

"Sorry, my friend. It's been a long day," Cain replied as he slumped down into the chair Morik had just vacated.

"Well, don't get too relaxed."

"I'll be fine."

"You'll have to tell me how you got those bruises later." Morik laughed as he patted Cain on the shoulder.

Cain sighed. "I'm sure you'll hear about it in short order."

"Right, well, have a good night down here," Morik said with a yawn, then disappeared up the ladder.

Cain watched him leave, then took a deep breath and let it out slowly. The stench no longer permeated the brig as it had when he first arrived on the ship. He couldn't tell if he was just getting used to it or if the forced air through the portholes had circulated it.

"Rough day?" a soft voice said.

Cain nodded and looked toward Lillia. She was watching him openly; her features had lost the harsh scowl she had carried since she arrived. His face brightened under her gaze.

"Seems to be going around lately," she said as she paced along the cell.

"You guys get into a fight?"

"Who, us?" Lillia asked, waving a hand at the repressed forms of the mages huddled around one another and whispering. "We do not have any fight left in us."

"I don't believe that," Cain replied. He stood and pulled the chair beside the cage and sat back down.

Lillia chuckled and stopped pacing. She looked at Cain levelly.

"Take yourself, for example. I can tell you have fire in your soul still; love burns deep, fueling your desire to return to Xonthian," Cain said with a shrug.

It was Lillia's turn to sigh. She slid down the bars to sit, but she said nothing, only stared at the wall of the brig. After several long moments, she finally spoke. "Until Den was born, I had never really known love. We loved him so much, and the love and devotion we showered on him he returned happily. But you never know true love until you have a child. Both my husband and I, we loved each other, but it was different, somehow filtered. It was laden with years of life, dulling our senses, building up walls around ourselves."

Cain listened intently, leaning forward to rest his elbows on his knees. The other mages, too, stopped whispering among themselves and listened, their collective eyes downcast in memory and loss.

"Mia was born a few years later. She came much easier than Den had. My husband and I used to joke that Den didn't want to come out, that he wasn't ready." A wry smile crept unbidden across her lips, her eyes staring into the past. Cain could tell she wasn't seeing him, the ship, or the bars. "Mia was like my husband—quiet, doting. Den was like me, ready to take on everyone and everything. When they were older, Den was fiercely protective of Mia. One day, they were playing outside, and I heard screaming. I ran outside and saw Den sitting on top of another boy; Mia was in tears. I pulled him off and asked what had happened, and he looked up at me with big round eyes and said, 'But mom, he tried to hug Mia!' The poor boy on the ground was crying and holding a broken flower."

Cain smiled at the picture and waited patiently for her to continue.

"We had a talk that night about being mean to people. That eventually Mia would grow up and find someone to love as we loved her." Lillia's eyes held unshed tears, as if storm clouds gathered there. Her mouth trembled and she set a hand on the crossbar as if steadying herself. "A few days later, the city guards showed up, and..."

Cain looked down at her and frowned. He clasped the bar beside her hand. He wanted to comfort her but didn't dare touch her unbidden. "Tell me what you did for a living."

"Huh?" She blinked as if Cain recalled her back to the present. Tears ran down her dirt-stained face, leaving behind a clean patch of skin. "What did I... Where did I work, you mean?"

"Yes," Cain said with a gentle smile.

She swallowed as if forcing down the bad memories of the past. "I worked at home, mostly. I made pottery. Because I could use fire so inherently, I'd mold the clay into pots, bowls, cups, and fire them when I was done. I'd sell them at the farmers market on the weekends."

"I bet you sold a lot."

"I... I guess I did." She smiled slightly, though happiness hadn't returned to her.

They sat awkwardly in silence for several moments, each lost in their thoughts. The mages behind her returned to their conversations. As Cain was about to stand, he felt a soft hand touch his.

"Thank you," Lillia whispered.

"For what?" Cain asked with a puzzled expression.

"For treating me like a human being and not like some freak of nature."

Cain stared into her eyes, pain and sorrow reflected back at him, though he couldn't be sure if it was hers or his he was seeing. He nodded solemnly and cupped her hand with his free one. "You're welcome."

Chapter 9

✦

DARKNESS BEFORE DAWN

"**H**EY, WERE YOU GOING to get up?" Goa shoved Cain to wake him, setting the hammock swinging.

Cain opened his weary eyes and looked at his friend. "Yeah, fine."

Goa chuckled and slid into the bottom hammock as Cain climbed out of his.

"Don't say I never did anything for you," Goa said with a laugh.

"Shhh, you'll wake everyone else," Cain hissed. He dressed and made his way to the main deck. The moon was settling down into the water, causing silver strands of light to glisten off the sea.

Waves lapped gently against the hull and echoed through the still night, although it was missing the usual brushing sound that accompanied it. He thought nothing of it, however, and took a deep, steady breath of the clean ocean air before heading down to the brig.

Morik greeted him with a yawn and a wave, then vanished back the way Cain had come.

The mages slept soundly, huddled near each other for comfort and safety. Cain sat down on the chair and stretched, a soft moan of satisfaction escaping his lips. As his muscles slowly released their tension, a loud thunk reverberated through the ship. He froze in place, looking toward the hull as if waiting for something to break through the wooden planks. Energy flowed through his body as his heart sped up, his palm turning sweaty as he groped for the dagger at his hip. His senses strained to detect anything out of the ordinary.

Cain rose from his chair guardedly and stood in front of the entry leading to the deck above. Something reminded him about the water, and he realized with a sudden rush of adrenaline they had stopped. They weren't moving, only bobbing up and down with the swells of the waves.

"What is it?" Lillia asked from the corner of the cell.

"Shhh," Cain hissed.

Cain set a foot on the first step of the ladder going up and froze. A shadow loomed above him, silhouetted against the starry sky. Before he could ask who was there, the figure fell through the hole. Cain tumbled out of the way, narrowly missing being hit. He drew his dagger and leveled it toward the body.

"Morik!?" Cain's eyes shot open as he examined the body. Blood pooled around him from a slit throat.

It was in that moment that the ship erupted with confusion, shouts, and orders. Cain looked up the ladder and saw an orange glow flickering, creating long shadows across the walls.

He pulled Morik's body aside and scrambled up the ladder. Unrecognizable shadows fought loudly in the chaos of the evening. He couldn't tell who was friend or foe in the fire-lit darkness. Everyone was obscured and disfigured by smoke and flame.

A boot appeared suddenly, momentarily distracting him. The heel of a shoe cracked against Cain's face, sending him tumbling back down the ladder. He fell to the deck below, his head hitting the hard teak deck with a sickening thunk. Stars danced in his narrowing vision as he tried to breathe. The sound of footfalls down the ladder was masked by the beating of his heart in his ears.

He heard voices, and a man appeared above him, holding the keys to the jail cell that had, up until this point, been hanging on the wall next to the chair.

The shadowy figure walked over to the cell and opened it, allowing the mages to pour out. The man appeared back at Cain's side, a sword pressed to his throat.

"No!" Lillia said, "I'll take care of him."

Cain's vision cleared enough to see the man above him nod and disappear up the ladder.

Lillia kneeled beside Cain and looked down at him with sorrow-filled eyes. Her warm hand grasped his. "I wish things had been different. I'm sorry."

"Me too," he croaked. Air flowed through his lungs as the shock of hitting the floor faded.

"Please, don't follow us. I don't want anything to happen to you." She touched his cheek and looked deep into his eyes.

He stared at her and knew she wasn't lying. "I... I would have followed you to the Fire Isles."

She closed her eyes as a tear slid down her cheek.

"We are leaving," a voice called down to them.

She stood and walked to the ladder, looking back at him briefly before ascending the rungs to the main deck above.

Cain willed his legs to move. He managed to roll over and pushed himself up. He shoved the pain of being kicked aside and forced his body to move. He wobbled to his feet and followed Lillia up the ladder.

His foot hit the main deck just as a scream pierced the night. He looked toward the sound and saw Coattes holding a dagger to Lillia's throat.

"No!" he yelled, and propelled himself forward, knocking the soldier and the mage to the deck. The dagger disappeared into the flames near the helm.

"How dare you!" Coattes screamed, rage contorting his face with hatred.

Before Coattes could attack Cain further, Lillia grabbed him by the arm, whispering something under her breath. Coattes's eyes flew open in horror. A silent scream erupted from his throat just as his head swelled. Steam roiled off his skin as it turned brown, then black, and he fell lifelessly to the ground.

Lillia looked at Cain and turned toward the waiting mages.

Cain took a step toward her, but a hand on his shoulder stopped him.

"No, stop," Goa said, his hands and face bloody.

Cain looked at him with sadness. He had known Goa most of his adult life. They had joined the ranks of the Swords of Justice together.

"I'm sorry," Cain said with downcast eyes, then walked toward the mages and Lillia.

Goa stood transfixed as the flames grew; the entire bridge was alight, as were the sails. Cain looked back one last time to see the betrayal and terror on Goa's face. Tears streamed down the strong man's cheeks, leaving trails of white in smudges of dirt and soot.

Cain turned away in shame and climbed down to the awaiting skiff, where the mages and their rescuers were waiting. Lillia gripped his hand and looked at him as he sat down. She said nothing. *She didn't need to,* he thought, *she knows what I felt. I did this to my friend and country what we had done to the mages—betrayed them.*

Chapter 10

YEAR ONE

Cain stood on the deck and stared at it. He felt numb, empty. Lillia walked over and clasped his trembling hand, squeezing it gently.

"How did this happen?" Cain asked softly.

"A few days before we were shipped out, we received word that there would be a rescue. I..." She paused and looked at him. "We didn't know it would be like this, I'm sorry."

Cain shook his head and turned to look at her. "No, it's I who should apologize. You were right. Right to be angry and hurt. What Xonthian did to you was unforgivable."

"You, too, lost loved ones," Lillia whispered.

Cain bowed his head as his brother's smiling face appeared in his memory. He pursed his lips and nodded.

"It's a start to something new, though; we'll fight for our loved ones. Our lost and fallen family," she said as she placed a finger under his chin and tilted his head up. "Be proud; you stand with us now."

Sailors and mages scurried around the deck, preparing to sail. Cain looked at them, then back at the burning wreckage in the distance.

"No one survived," an aged, powerful voice said behind them.

Cain turned with Lillia. A man, dressed as the captain, bowed low before them. His skin was silky white, even in the pre-dawn light that fought back the darkness at the edge of the world.

"I must retire for the day; it's been a long night. But I wanted to welcome you aboard... Who should I say I have the pleasure of meeting?" he asked cordially.

"My name is Cain. This is Lillia," he said with a bow.

"Ah, welcome aboard. My name is Sengue Bebedor," the captain said with a grin. "You, my friend Cain, are not a mage, are you?"

"I am not, sir."

"Well, then, why are you on my ship?"

Cains eyes widened slightly.

"He's with me, sir," Lillia said shakily, her hand holding Cain's tighter.

"Ah, love," Sengue said silkily. "I'm afraid, though, love has no place in my war."

"I don't understand. Who are we at war..." Cain fell silent as Sengue suddenly loomed in front of him.

The captain's hand grasped Cain's head, forced it to the side, and bit his neck. Lillia screamed, her hand still grasping Cain's. Sengue sucked vigorously, then backed away. Blood dripped down the man's lips and chin. A smile of content spread across his face.

"You will be my first general, Cain. Thank you for your sacrifice," Sengue said triumphantly. "It's fitting that it be a soldier from the Swords of Justice."

His laugh echoed through the last bit of darkness before the sun rose in the distance. Sengue Bebedor turned toward the captain's quarters, leaving Cain standing shakily on the deck of the ship. His eyes had glazed over, not quite dead but also not quite alive. Lillia cried in shock and fear beside him.

Battle
of
Smoke and Fire

Chapter 1

CROSS ROADS

ROARIC SLID ACROSS THE wooden bench, his hood pulled low over his face, concealing his features from those looking at him. The men across the table were similarly cloaked in shadows and leaned forward. They greeted him with a curt nod and only the barest of glances. The stench of unwashed bodies and thick smoke hung in the air around them.

"You're right, the clerics are shipping the mages out through South Kelsa," Roaric whispered, running his hand along the edge of the table as he shifted into a comfortable position. The oak table was worn smooth from use.

The younger man looked around nervously. "Quiet, someone might hear you."

Roaric gritted his teeth in irritation. He glanced over his shoulder at the uproar behind him. Men and women celebrating gods knew what danced and sang with such merriment no one could hear the three conspirators in the corner. He turned his attention back to the two men at the table and ignored the younger man's agitation.

"Roaric, are you sure we have the support of the others?" Dall, the older man fidgeting with the hem of his cloak, asked and fixed him with a somber look.

"I am. We'll set off in the morning," Roaric replied with a grin.

The barmaid stepped over to their table and sat down three mugs of ale. "Here ya go, fella's. Enjoy."

The Cross Roads Tavern and Inn sat between North and South Kelsa along a stretch of road that split east toward Xonthian City. It was a major resting point for traders moving goods around the western continent. The tavern was well-worn, homey, and felt welcoming despite the ebb and flow of guests that wet their lips and filled their bellies.

The Cross Roads was a small establishment, and although several people were living on the lands, it was more of a compound than any type of village. It consisted of a tavern, inn, stables, gardens, and two houses where the groundskeepers lived.

Roaric watched her disappear through the crowd before taking a mug and swallowing a mouth full of the warm, stale liquid. "Come now, Dall, Quil, drink up. We'll meet at the stables in the morning."

The tavern was well lit from candles to the fireplace, filling the space with warm, stuffy air that mingled with the already pungent body odors.

Quil shot Dall a sidelong glance before raising the mug to his lips. Roaric watched as the young man took a swig, grimaced at the taste, and then coughed.

"Better get used to worse than this, my boy," Roaric said before taking another swallow. "You'll be begging for this luxury before we're through."

"If you want to free our brothers and sisters, better grow some hair on your chest," Dall said, nudging the young man with a wink, although Roaric noticed there was no humor in his expression.

"Are you not afraid of being caught?" Quil asked.

"I fear worse things than what judgment men may hand down upon us," Roaric said, emptying his mug and slamming it down. "I'll see you two in the morning. Get some rest; the ride south will be long." Roaric stood and made his way through the jovial crowd that lingered near the fireplace and disappeared down the corridor toward the rooms.

Roaric lifted an arm off his chest. The women that lay on either side of him moaned and shifted. The sun seeped through the thin muslin curtains. The smell of whiskey and smoke from the kitchen wafted in from under the door. As he climbed over the blond beside him, he kissed her deeply. The taste of last night's wine still lingered on her lips. The brunette on the other side pouted as she stretched out under the heavy blanket. He grinned and kissed her in turn.

"I must be off," Roaric said as he climbed out of the bed to sit beside them. "You two behave."

They shushed him and snuggled together, waving a dismissing hand in illustration.

He smiled and stood, then dressed and quietly left through the room's only door. He made his way through the nearly empty common room to the cool morning air. He crossed the dirt path to the stables on the other side, where Dall and Quil were waiting.

Roaric returned his gaze to the men before him and saw how dark their eyes were, heavy from lack of sleep.

"You're late," Dall growled.

"Sorry, I had some business last night I had to take care of," he said with a smirk.

Merchants hitched horses to wagons while shouting rushed orders to their crews of guards and horsemen. Stable hands roamed around with various harnesses and blankets for the animals waiting in their pens. The atmosphere felt sluggish, mirroring the weary resignation of the men waiting for him. A thick, oppressive silence hung in the air, heavy with the weight of unspoken worries and exhausted patience.

Dell glared at him but said nothing. He handed Roaric the reins to a horse. "Are you ready?" he asked, his eyes heavy.

"Aye." His expression hardened. "Do you have everything we'll need?"

Dall nodded and jutted his chin toward his mount. A saddle bag straddled the mare's haunches.

The three men mounted their horses and directed them south. The Cross Roads disappeared as horse hooves thundered along the hard-packed road. A cool, crisp breeze washed over them, bringing with it the smell of grass and peat. Roaric focused ahead, his jaw set against the constant jolting rhythm of the horse's trot.

Chapter 2

◄─○─►

COLD FLICKER

Fog hung thick in the early morning air. The sun hadn't yet broken over the rim of the Xonthian Mountains to the east. Roaric shivered, pulling his cloak tighter over his shoulders. Dall and Quil lay in their bedrolls, oblivious to the grim pre-dawn sky. The horses were tethered to a tree a few feet behind them, concealed from the road just a few yards away.

Despite the crispness around him, the smell was soothing. They hadn't started a campfire for fear of being seen, which kept smoke from clogging his nostrils. He stood and paced the small clearing in hopes of warming his limbs. His footfalls crunched under his heels, causing Dall to wake up and peer at him with a furrowed brow.

"Is it morning?"

"No," Roaric replied.

The aging man groaned and sat up, drawing his bed roll up over his shoulders. His pale blue eyes watched Roaric as he continued to pace.

"Cold or anxious?" Dall finally asked.

Roaric stopped and grinned at the older man, though the edges of his smile didn't feel believable. "It's colder than Icesis's tits."

Dall snorted derisively. "Who are we expecting with this caravan?" Dall asked.

"The king and clerics of Gate'har have been sending acolytes. I don't see why we wouldn't expect that to continue, at least in the short term."

Dall nodded in agreement.

"If they start sending knights, or worse, paladins, then we'll worry," Roaric added.

The sound of horse hooves approaching caused the hair on his arms to prickle with warning. Dall nudged Quil awake as he stood, tossing the bedroll to the side. Quil grunted then stood, jolted awake by the sound of a horse growing close.

"Hail, traveler, a fine morning," the rider said. "You happen to have a fire to warm my toes?"

"No, but we have mittens," Roaric replied.

The rider nodded and dropped down from his saddle, extending a hand to Roaric. "Well met, friend."

"And you." Roaric turned to the others, clapping the rider on the shoulder. "Gentlemen, this is Manso. Now, tell me rider, what news do you bring?"

"The caravan is about two hours behind me. Ten Gate'har acolyte guards; two of them are crossbowmen."

Roaric nodded. "The crossbowmen will be our first target then. Quil, get the gear from the horses. Let's get started."

Quil returned a moment later with a pile of netting under each arm. Roaric led them back to the road as the sun illuminated the eastern sky. Its warm rays started to whisk the shroud of fog away, giving the impression the gods were watching them.

The men split into two groups; each group rolled netting across the road and concealed it under dirt, leaves, and grass, setting it to spring up with a single pull of a rope. Once completed, they waited behind trees and shrubs, leaving a lingering silence to grow between them. After half an hour, the sound of metal clanking mixed with the pounding of hooves on hard-packed dirt startled them from their reverie.

Roaric's heart thundered in his chest in time with the caravan march. He glanced toward Manso, who was nearby; Quil and Dall were farther down the road. As the lead soldiers drew close to the nets, they pulled the rope dangling from the tree. It snapped taut, pulling the rigging up and trapping the troops between them. Before they could react, Roaric and Manso stood and bellowed curses as they ran toward the Gate'har acolytes. A bolt from the crossbowmen farther down the line whistled by. Roaric ducked, but it wouldn't have mattered. If he could hear it, it would have been too late. He leapt at one of the riders and pulled him down, stabbing him in the side with a dagger as he did. He glanced down the road and saw the crossbowmen falling to the ground as Quil and Dall slit their throats.

Roaric picked up a spear and launched it at an acolyte who was spurring his horse toward him. The weapon buried itself in the man's chest and sent him flying off the back of the creature.

He ran over to the soldier's spear and picked it up, dodging the tip of another as he did. The two remaining acolytes yelled at each other. Their commands were unclear to Roaric as blood and adrenaline pumped through his veins. They reined their horses around and took off around the netting.

Cheers from the captured wagon drowned out the death throes of dying men on the road, causing Roaric to shift his attention to the shackled prisoners. Dall walked over to them with Quil close behind. Manso tossed the elder man a set of keys from one of the dead soldiers.

Roaric walked over to one of the acolytes that lay wounded on the ground.

The man's eyes were narrowed in hatred. "Go on, finish it."

"I will," Roaric replied, kneeling beside him. "Answer me this though. Why would Gate'har choose this for her children? Would she banish those with magic like fresh meat to be tossed?"

The soldier grit his teeth but said nothing.

Roaric nodded, his lips pursed, and pulled the soldier's knife from his belt, studying it a moment before plunging it into the man's heart.

Roaric stood with a heavy sigh and turned toward the growing crowd of liberated mages from the wagon. Manso walked over to him and clasped his shoulder in a job well done. One of the mages stepped over to Roaric and extended a hand.

"Thank you," the grime-covered woman said. Her black hair was matted and clumped in ropes.

"You're welcome. Hurry and gather your kin, we need to get off the road before others find us."

"Of course," she replied, and began to turn. She stopped and peered back at Roaric.

"You didn't use any magic to save us. Are you not a mage?"

Roaric shook his head. "No, we're not mages. Just men who feel there is injustice in the king's and clerics' decision to exile your kind."

She furrowed her brows at him but nodded anyway. Clearly, she had questions. Before she asked anything further, she returned to the wagon and ushered the captured away from the gruesome rescue.

Roaric watched as Dall and Quil led them toward camp. They would need to leave, and the closest, easiest place to disappear was South Kelsa. Despite the victory of their first attempt, he was well aware this was only the beginning. He only prayed to whatever gods were listening they all would go as easily.

Chapter 3

SMOLDERING ASH

ROARIC SLID DOWN FROM his saddle to the soft earth of the street. His boots sunk into the mud with a soft squishing sound. The city hummed with rhythms of commerce, while workers farther away at the docks could be heard shouting orders. He handed the reins of his horse to the stable boy standing beside the beast, rubbing a soothing hand along the creature's flank.

"Thanks, kid," Roaric said.

"Of course, sir."

Roaric watched as the others dismounted and collected their things before heading into the inn a few feet away. The crowd of mages slid inside without a word. Their grim faces were drained and hollow from lack of sleep from the long hike to South Kelsa and the stresses of being taken from their homes.

He followed them inside and found a table for himself and the three other liberators while the refugees settled in around them. Their heads bowed together as they whispered fearfully.

"Well," Dall began, sitting across from Roaric. "Now what?"

Manso and Quil joined them, their eyes settling on Roaric in expectation of a response to Dall's question.

He took a deep breath and let it out slowly before responding. "We can't stay here long; the crown and the church both will be sending inquisitors in search of their missing mages."

"And you have a boat for them?" Manso asked.

"Yes. More or less," he replied.

Dall raised an eyebrow in question.

"The captain of the ship is supposed to be in town here, I've not met him, and the ship they were promised was a Merc vessel," Roaric said, looking around the room as if looking for the man in question. Although, all he wanted now was a drink. "Where is the barmaid?"

"Mercs, Roaric? For god's sake, you might as well send them back to Xonthian City," Dall said, shaking his head before sitting back in his chair.

Quil looked between the two men, his brow furrowed in confusion. Manso caught the expression and put a hand on the younger man's shoulder to quell any questions he might have started to ask.

"Look, it was short notice, and well, I hadn't really figured out that part. I was in a hurry," Roaric replied.

"You had months to plan this attack; what do you mean you didn't have time?" Dall asked with a slight growl in his voice.

Roaric gritted his teeth; he wanted to yell at the older man but thought better of it. He needed a drink. Several, in fact.

"You were busy whoring around, weren't you? If you didn't want to be here, you shouldn't have brought us all together."

"Don't be a fool, old man. You know damn well my intentions in this are purely for-" He trailed off as the barmaid approached.

The woman's grimy features reflected the state of the town and the inn they currently sat in. She had a dry smile, one that meant she had served her share of hardened individuals. "What can I get you, gentlemen?"

"Whiskey, and ale. A lot of the latter," Roaric stated with an edge in his voice that caused the woman to purse her lips. He cursed himself for being overly irritated.

"Of course. And the rest?"

They gave their orders and waited for her to leave before continuing their conversation.

"What is the deal with Mercs?" Quil asked as he turned to Dall.

"They are notorious for selling their loyalty to the highest bidder. They'd sell their own mother and slit her throat for the right price," Dall said.

"The Mercs were the only ones willing to risk the journey north. Are they smugglers? No, but the Anarchs are a lot more expensive. And in case you aren't aware, I'm not made of money," Roaric muttered.

"Now that you mention it, I don't believe we've ever spoken about why you are even doing this. What are you getting out of it?" Manso asked.

"Why are any of us? Because what's happening is horrible. Why would I need ulterior motives?"

Manso shrugged and sipped from his mug, eyeing Roaric.

Roaric let out a slow, even breath, not realizing he had been holding it. He glanced away as if something caught his attention away from others' penetrating stare.

The barmaid brought the men their drinks and disappeared again to help some of the refugees. Roaric took the whiskey and swallowed it whole. Its smokey, warm flavor burned its way down his throat. He hissed in euphoric pain before setting the glass down and taking a swig of ale.

"I need to go find the Merc and get their passage squared away," Roaric said. He finished the mug of ale and stood. He tossed a few coins on the table and turned toward the door.

Roaric rolled over onto the bed beside the woman, letting out a grunt of exhaustion. "By the gods," he said, a smile of contentment splitting his lips.

The woman giggled and propped herself up on one elbow before running a finger down Roaric's heaving chest, slick with moisture.

"I need a minute to catch my breath," he said, peering into her bright amber eyes. "Are all of you mages this talented?"

"Only the most thankful of us," she whispered sultrily. She leaned over him and kissed him deeply.

The taste of ale on her lips mixed with the musk of sex that permeated the room. He ran a hand through her hair and held it tightly.

She pulled back and smiled mischievously. "Is that enough incentive to keep going?"

A wide grin spread across his face, and he rolled over on top of her, pulling her tightly to him. His muscular frame pinned her down, soliciting wild giggles from her as he did. "Woman, you'll be the death of me," he said, before attacking her lips fervently with his. The wood bed groaned under their weight and movement. The thin headrest, simple in its construction, banged into the wall as her laughter melted into moans of pleasure. The small room echoed with their passion and the sound of the furniture straining against their lust.

When they were done, Roaric melted once more into the matted hay mattress, a moan of relief escaping his lips. She echoed his fulfillment and snuggled into the crook of his arm as they drifted into slumber.

Chapter 4

THE VANISHED

R OARIC TOOK A DEEP breath of the morning air. The smell of pine mixed with the musty, wet earth around the camp. Vines snaked through the lower branches of birch, pine, and willows, giving them a sense of being embraced by nature. He peered around the makeshift hideout; lean-tos made up most of the shelters around the camp, with a single, larger structure in the center.

He walked over to the building and stepped inside, greeting Dall and Quil as he did. Manso looked up from the missives he was pouring over on the table in the center of the room, giving him a curt nod.

"As expected, they have increased security along the road. These last few months of hitting the caravans have finally prompted a response from the king. He's ordered the garrison at Port Orlynns to take up station in South Kelsa to provide support," Manso said, sliding a sheet of paper towards Roaric.

"Our friends in the smuggler's cove won't like the increased shipping patrols," Dall pointed out.

Talli, one of the mages they rescued recently, a thin, malnourished-looking woman with sunken, grey eyes, entered the war room, plopping down into a makeshift chair. The men greeted her, then turned back to the letters on the table.

"I've been hearing rumbles that more and more mages want to go to the Fire Isles," Talli said with a shake of her head.

"Why in all hells would they want to go there?"

"I've been hearing whispers about a growing resistance there," she replied.

Roaric read the missive and tossed it back on the table. "Be that as it may, we'll be fine. Our numbers have grown. We'll handle the increased caravan guards."

The Mercs had built a small dock east of the South Kelsa, hidden from sight in the rocky shores that ran farther east. From there, a sloop waited to take the rescued mages to either Xecutran or Juan'kij, depending on storms along the coast.

"Eventually, we may not need to rescue them if the word keeps spreading to all mages," Talli said with a shrug.

"Roaric, it's not just the increased manpower that has me worried. We're no longer able to do this without major combat training," Dall said.

Roaric nodded in agreement. "None of us are trained soldiers, but I agree with you. Manso, any suggestions?" The two of them were the closest to fighters they had. Manso once worked as a guard for merchant caravans, and Roaric had been a Merc.

Manso tapped his fingers on the table and glanced around at the gathered men. "I could train anyone with using a spear, or shield. But I suspect we'll need more than that."

"Run some drills with the recruits. Talli, do you think you could support us with magic?" Roaric asked.

"I'm not here for my health," she muttered.

"Good, then we'll meet up at the ambush spot in the morning," he said, nodding with finality. He watched as the assembled made their way out of the room, leaving only Talli behind.

Her cold, calculating eyes watched him a moment before she too stood. "Ever wonder how this ends?"

"I suspect with our necks tied to a noose in Xonthian City," he replied.

"If we're so lucky," she said, before disappearing out of the door.

Roaric yawned. His eyelids were heavy, not from lack of sleep but from soul-draining boredom. The caravan was expected an hour ago, at least that's what Manso had told them. He sat against a tree, trying to keep his eyes focused on the road a few feet away. No one spoke, leaving the soothing songs of birds to lull him further into relaxation.

As he gave in and closed his eyes, he heard hooves approaching, causing him to snap wide awake. He shifted to a kneeling position, his sword gripped in one hand, a shield in the other. He glanced along the path to see Quil, Dall, and Manso similarly poised to strike. He knew Talli and two others were on the opposite side.

As the caravan approached, he heard a warning from the horse riders. They had seen someone.

Roaric growled and sprang toward them. He slammed into the first acolyte he saw, causing him to fall off the horse and land with a loud thud. The horse beside him had a chance to stab toward Roaric, but the spear tip glanced off the round shield.

An explosion from behind the column of riders shattered the already chaotic atmosphere around them and setting everything ablaze. Roaric wondered idly why it was delayed; something was off. He shifted his attention back to the second acolyte and twisted away from a spear thrust. Roaric lunged at the rider with his sword, piercing him in his side and causing blood to gush in a river of crimson.

Roaric heard screams coming from farther away, and he turned and bolted for the shouts. As he came around the wagon, he saw a Gate'har knight holding Talli by the throat and fighting off Quil with her free hand.

The knight outmatched Quil. Her horse lay dead nearby as the young man tried to fight the more experienced warrior.

"Quil! Back off!" Roaric yelled.

Roaric sprinted toward the knight, his sword held out beside him like a serpent ready to strike. Quil barely moved out of the way as the knight's sword came crashing down where the young man's head had been a moment earlier.

The knight turned in time to see Roaric approach. She looked down at Talli in her iron grip. From his current distance, Roaric could see the pain and fear in the mage's face as the knight's grasp tightened.

With lightning reflexes, the knight slammed her fist with the sword into the mage's face. Talli's head snapped back. Blood poured from the woman's throat, and a tear where the knight had been holding her began to flow with blood.

"Quil, get Talli out of here!" Roaric said as he swung his sword horizontally at the knight.

The knight glared at Roaric as she turned her attention toward him, his blade easily parried aside. Fiery ice-blue eyes pierced his, a mask of anger and hatred clear in her features framed by short auburn hair.

Roaric glanced over his shoulder as he saw the remaining rebels finish off the last few guards. Quil had dragged Talli away, leaving the knight and Roaric to face off against one another. He turned his attention to her, putting himself between the knight and the wagon that contained the prisoners.

"You're not a mage," she growled.

"No, I am not," he replied. His hands flexed, his knuckles turning white with the strain of holding a sword and shield. He scanned her as they positioned themselves around one another. The armor she wore was decorated with the Knights of Gate'har crest, one of the higher rankings of the clerics. He would have grinned at the rebel's growing notoriety if she wasn't glaring at him with such loathing and condemnation.

The knight noticed his gap in concentration and exploited it. She lunged at him, her sword intent on skewering him. He barely deflected the blow with his shield. She kept on him, however, and swung with growing intensity. He didn't need to beat her, he just had to survive long enough for the others to free the mages and disappear.

His shield arm began to ache as the wood cracked and splintered apart from the relentless attacks. Roaric gritted his teeth against the growing pain. He tried to parry some of the attacks, but she was fast and relentless.

He shot glances around, looking for an escape but seeing none. He heard shouts from Manso somewhere nearby. The mages had been freed, but it was the shouts that sounded like a command that caught his attention.

Roaric deflected the knight's sword, and before he could attack, movement in the corner of his eye told him he needed to look. As he turned to face it, the cart tilted backward in a violent crack of wood. The horses pulling the wagons bayed in protest. Roaric had enough time to dash out of the way before it crashed backward toward the knight. Free of the weight, the horses bolted down the road.

Without thinking, Roaric took the distraction to bolt for the woods, away from the knight. He glanced to the other side and saw the shadows of the rebels melt into the dense woodland farther away. His heart pounded loudly in his ears as he realized they had narrowly escaped. He heard a woman scream in rage in the knight's direction. Blood and adrenaline rushed through his veins as a smile spread across his face.

Chapter 5

COLD FIRE

SEVERAL DAYS AGO.

Sannoa walked fervently down the marble corridor towards the citadel's central transept. Rows of dark wood pews sat empty in neat columns facing the asp near the northern section of the temple.

Hearing her heavy footfalls echoing through the chamber, an elderly man in silver and gold robes looked up. He sat the book he was flipping through down on the alter. The grey platform was etched with a crown of gold stars signifying the Gate'har Goddess; under those was an ankh, a symbol of life.

"Ah, Sannoa, what can I do for you?" the cleric asked.

"You sent Terk to Xonthian City? Why?" she asked. She glared at him. She felt the heat radiating from her as the words escaped her lips. Her voice reverberated through the massive, vaulted room.

The cleric raised an eyebrow at her. "Calm your voice, the gods can hear you just fine."

She clenched her jaw in irritation.

"To your point, however, Terk was selected because he-"

"Because HE has a cock between his legs," she said, cutting him off.

"Your insinuation that Terk was sent because he's a man has no basis here."

"Bullshit."

The cleric rolled his eyes. "Sannoa, child, your time will come to serve in the Goddess's name. Continue to pray and study, and the time will come."

Sannoa clenched her fists before spinning on her heel and storming off. She had to get away before she said something she would regret.

Sannoa stood among the wreckage of the caravan. The stench of burnt flesh from the horse mingled with the wet, moldy smell of earth. One of her acolytes groaned in pain nearby. A broken spear tip protruded from the man's stomach.

"Please... Sister... Heal me," he said, tears of pain trailing down his mud-caked face.

Sannoa knelt beside him and placed a hand on the broken spear handle. She set her face in a grim expression and twisted, then pushed the spear up into the man's heart. His last breath hissed from the gushing wound in a bloody gurgle.

She walked over to the mage she had killed; they had left her behind. "Wise," she said. She looked in the direction the rebels had disappeared before turning to her horse, where she pulled off leather riding bags. While they were singed, the leather had held off the flames, she hoped it was enough to save its contents from destruction.

She opened the flap and looked inside. Basic camping gear, flint, whetstone, oil, small amount of rope, and some dried meat and fruit. Everything was there. She closed the bag and pulled the bedroll from a dead horse that wasn't burned up. She tied it to the bag and slung it over her shoulder. She sheathed her sword and stepped into the forest on the side of the road the rebels had disappeared. Her cold blue eyes scanned the ground as she went. While the trees and brush had hidden their escape, they left a large enough swath of trampled ferns, making it easy to follow them.

Sannoa muttered under her breath as she pushed through the underbrush. While the rebels had left a clear trail, they were light enough to keep branches from snapping. They left very few footprints behind in a several places, as grass and smaller brush was bouncing back. Her heavy plate and chainmail armor, however, crashed through everything like a startled horse through the streets.

After several hours of hiking through the densely-packed thickets and sparse grassy clearings, the trail of boots multiplied and focused along simple game trail heading south. She followed those, a sense of purpose renewing in her veins. Anger began to prickle her skin once again, and she thought of ways she would attack the rebels.

It was the latter that caused her to momentarily pause in her pursuit. How would she assault them? It was only her now; she had no backup. There were at least a half dozen of them, including mages. She growled and turned around to look where she had come from.

"Fuck," she mumbled. She had already trudged miles through the forest after them. Even if she did turn back, she wasn't sure she could find her way.

She set her jaw and continued her pursuit. She pushed her way through the trees to another clearing. The tall grass, green with life but as tall as her waist, slowed her progress. She lost the trail she had been following. She glanced around, and as she did, movement caught her attention. She pulled her sword and faced it. More movement, repeated by a third.

"Show yourself!" she said, shifting her weight from one patch of movement to the other. Whatever it was drew closer. The hair on her neck prickled in mute warning, urging her to run.

She pushed the feeling down. Instinct told her to turn around, and as she did, the pinchers of a horse-sized spider snapped at her. She barely moved enough to keep from losing her head. She rolled out of the way but lost her bag in the process. Three other spiders, smaller but faster, scurried from the brush toward her. She swung at the closest and managed to cut off one of its outstretched legs. Two others pressed their assault toward her, thrusting their mandibles at her in rapid succession. She stabbed one and barely managed to wrest the blade from its thick armor plating before it scurried off. Sannoa glanced over her shoulder and saw the game trail at the edge of the forest. She turned and bolted for the thicker, denser-packed forest, keeping the path in sight as she ran. She cursed herself for losing the saddle bags as she burst through the vines and underbrush.

She turned, expecting the spiders to follow, but she saw them fade back in the direction they had come. She shook her head and sheathed her sword. "Damnit," she mumbled, and continued her search for the rebels. Sannoa was not fond of nature, and she wasn't trained in living hard in the forests of Xonthian. She suddenly missed being home in eastern Xonthian, in the deserts and lowlands around her home. Where the things that tried to kill you could be spotted among the rocks and dry sage. The forest, she felt, gave false security. She only hoped she could make it out alive.

Chapter 6

SMOKE IN THE CAMP

S HADOWS GREW LONG, ENGULFING the floor of the woods in darkness as the sun began to set. Time marked on, and Sannoa questioned the wisdom of running after the mercenaries who had attacked her caravan. Her footfalls were loud to her as her armor made metal clanking sounds. She grew more anxious with each step.

Something caught her attention, and she froze in place. The smoke of dampened campfire hung in the air, signaling her approach to the rebel's highway deep in the forest. She knelt behind a large pine tree and strained her senses. Other than the smell of smoke, there was nothing else she could discern. No sound of men talking, no dogs barking. Someone coughed in the near distance, causing her heart to leap into her throat. She plastered herself against the tree and frantically looked around. After several tense moments, no one came and she peeled herself away from the bark, cautiously moving forward.

A few yards away, a circle of tents was masked by vines and branches and strewn with leaves. The area was camouflaged carefully in the woods, giving the rebels a new, perfect place to hide. Men and women sat around a central campfire. No one spoke, their heads bowed in silent contemplation. She started to move, but the metal on her armor clinked, and again she froze. Her heart pounded loudly in her ears.

Sannoa had to get out of the heavy, bulky armor. There was no way she could attack them here anyway. She had to find a way out first. She muttered silently to herself and quietly removed her plate armor and heavy chain under armor, leaving only her leather jerkin, breeches, and braces. She hung her sword over her shoulder so it was firmly strapped to her, rather than dangling beside her. When she was done, she hid her armor as best she could under a clump of vines growing around the tree.

She circled the camp until she found what looked to be a well-traveled path running south. She hid behind a tree on one side as one of the fighters she had seen at the ambush came out of a tent across the clearing from her. He was talking with an older man, while a younger one shuffled beside them. She wished she could hear what was being said. She sat back against the tree. All she could do now is wait.

"We can't leave Talli out there," Dall said, slamming his fist down on the table.

Roaric ran a hand through his greasy hair and looked at the older man. "Look, we can't go back, either. That'd expose us." He stood and walked to the tent flap and ducked outside. Dall and Quil followed him outside.

"Talli was one of us, she-"

"Enough, Dall, we can't. I'm sorry. We have an entire camp here just under a day's walk to the road. Any one of those soldiers we left alive back there could potentially find us. We can't risk bringing them directly here by carrying a dead body. Besides, when we got her back, what would we do with her? Huh? Bury her here under a tree in an unmarked grave?"

"So leave her rotting on the road for the wolves?"

"That road isn't exactly empty; someone will find all those bodies eventually. Better to leave them there than risk dragging her corpse back," Roaric said, glaring at the man. "Look around, we have a caravan of mages hiding here right now. Bringing the body back and attracting attention would bring all of Gate'har's knights down on us."

Dall pursed his lips but didn't say anything.

"I know you mean well, but we can't risk it," Roaric said with a heavy sigh. "Get some rest. I'll be heading out tomorrow for the city. We need supplies. Quil, as soon as light breaks, take the mages south to the rendezvous with the smugglers. Dall and Manso will stay here and keep guard."

"All right," Quil said, and shuffled off to his tent.

Roaric looked at Dall, who was still watching him. He raised a brow at the older man and opened his mouth to retort but said nothing instead. Roaric shook his head and headed back to the tent to find something to wash his face. The dust of battle weighed heavily on him. Although he wasn't sure if it was that or Talli's death.

The morning fog hung low in the boughs of the trees. The sun sent rays of orange spears through it as it spread its warmth across the forest. Sannoa hugged her knees close in an attempt to keep warm throughout the long, cold evening. Her jaw ached from her constant shivering. The moss and leaves she wrapped around her shoulders did very little to keep the biting cold of the night away.

She heard footfalls and saw the man who, to her, appeared to be the rebels' leader. The younger man she heard called Quil followed him out, along with the group of mages they had freed the day before. She waited until the camp was quiet once again and followed the leader.

The rush of adrenaline warmed her limbs as she moved. She watched from the shadows of trees as the man hiked along the game trail. Her confidence building, she thought she could take them. The surprise alone would ensure that. But she wasn't so sure of herself that he wouldn't just be replaced. She had to find reinforcements in South Kelsa. Their stay of execution was a tenacious one, and with each hour that passed, she reevaluated the decision. When she saw signs of civilization as the sun set, she knew her victory was assured.

Chapter 7

MAKING DO

South Kelsa smelled as it always did—trash mixed with rotten fish. It wasn't the worst thing Roaric had smelled; that was reserved for a childhood memory he had of finding unidentifiable puss seeping out of a festering wound on the family dog. The poor creature had to be put down after that.

He pulled the door to the tavern open and walked inside. The smell of stew, stale ale, and unwashed bodies assaulted him. It smelled far better than the stench of decay outside.

"Ale, please. And a bowl of that stew, if there's any left," Roaric said, sliding a few silver coins toward the barkeep.

"Aye, of course," the elder man said as he began to pour the liquid into a recently washed cup.

"Any news?" Roaric asked as he took the offered drink.

"More dead acolytes on the road north, merchant found them on his way in apparently," he replied, sliding a bowl of bread over toward Roaric.

"Damn shame."

"Aye, well, not sure Gate'har will see it that way. I heard the mages are starting to gather in the Fire Isles. Strange place for them, if ya ask me," the barkeep said, before disappearing into the kitchen.

Roaric took a piece of the hard bread and gnawed on it thoughtfully. The idea of the mages going to the Fire Isles was lost on him. Why anyone would willingly go there and join the rest of the exiles was beyond his comprehension. The islands were not hospitable and, from what he knew, were barely able to sustain life.

"Here ya go. Anything else I can getcha?" the barkeep asked.

"Aye, looking for a room and some company for the evening," Roaric said as he plopped the bread into the offered stew.

"Well then, I have just the thing for you," the man said with a wide grin as he signaled to a woman standing a few feet away.

Sannoa had only been to South Kelsa once before. Like the last trip, this one was looking unappealing as well. She saw the rebel leader disappear into the tavern. She didn't need to keep tabs on him now, though; she knew where they were hiding.

She stormed toward the garrison, situated near the docks, and barged into the office, surprising an older man dressed in a modest soldier uniform.

"I need some of your best men," she said as she entered.

After he composed himself from her sudden appearance, he looked her over. She realized suddenly she wasn't wearing her armor any longer and felt naked from his probing gaze. She shook it off and glared at him.

"I'm sorry, who are you?" he asked.

"Sannoa of the Knights of Gate'har, Second Legion of the Goddess," she replied, trying to force the irritation down.

"Ah, you are alive. I heard your caravan had been attacked. I just recently took the statement from the merchant who had found it," he replied as he shuffled through the papers on the desk in front of him. "Ah, here it is. I could amend this, I suppose."

"Fine, do that, I just need men. I know where the attackers are hiding; we can shut down their operation," she said.

"I'm sorry, whom are you referring to?" the soldier asked, raising a brow.

Sannoa's face flushed as anger bubbled over. "You backwoods, lazy slob of a soldier. The REBELS that are attacking us every time we bring a batch of magi scum down here for processing."

The soldier just watched her, as if she had suddenly sprouted a second head and was speaking a foreign language.

Sannoa took a deep breath and leaned down to look levelly into the man's eyes. "I am taking a group of your best men tomorrow morning. I will use them to hunt down the criminals that have been ambushing Gate'har caravans for months. Do you have a problem with this?"

He shook his head.

"Good," she said, and stood upright. "Now show me where your armory is."

Chapter 8

SMOTHERED MATE

GETTING THE MEN IN line to march took longer than expected. However, Sannoa knew she couldn't follow the rebel leader back to his camp. With the dozen men she had at her back, they would have been noticed far too soon. The weather threatened to drown them in rain, a prospect that weighed on her as much as the mud would if they had to slog through the woods.

She wasn't surprised at the eagerness of the selected soldiers to hunt down those attacking the caravans. The men and women she selected were scarred, thick-skinned, and gruff looking. Their armor wasn't the most pristine she had ever seen, but that didn't surprise her. She wasn't in Xonthian City.

The armor she selected to temporarily replace the stately armor she lost did little to cover vital areas of her arms and torso. It was small and barely gave her enough room to move. She muttered as she tried to straighten it for the hundredth time.

She recognized some of the flora and fauna and realized they were getting closer. She brought the men to a halt and formed them into a semi-circle before giving them the signal to move out.

Sannoa slid her sword from its sheath as quietly as she could. When the camp was visible through the thick brush, she shouted a charge, and the men burst into the camp. They tore into tents and burst through lean-tos, scattering wood and canvas as they went.

She stood in the center, watching the chaos slowly fade. The hair on her arms prickled as her heart rate suddenly spiked. It was a trap.

"Damn, woman. You sure do know how to make an entrance," a voice called from the trees behind her. She whirled around to see the man she knew as the rebel leader stroll into the camp. His hand rested on the hilt of a sword, currently sheathed on his hip.

"You!" she said, leveling her sword at him. She looked him over; the man's features held a certain amount of confidence. His short brown hair was combed back, giving her a clear view of his sharp grey eyes.

The soldiers closest to him started to advance but froze as he raised a hand. "You might want to wait a moment, lads," he said, pointing toward the edge of the camp. Several men stood with bows drawn, pointed toward them.

Sannoa glared at him. "Who will I have the pleasure of buring, once this is all over?"

"My name is Roaric," he bowed mockingly, sweeping his hand nearly to the ground. "And you are?"

"Death," she growled.

Roaric chuckled.

"You're in no position to dictate this skirmish. While you have us surrounded, we are far better equipped to defeat you," Sannoa said.

"Oh, I know that. I was thinking, though, maybe we could work this out, you and me, before this devolved into conflict."

"Why would I want to do that? Did you consider that when you attacked my caravan and murdered those acolytes?" Sannoa asked.

"Valid point. Though, I'm just stalling you," Roaric said as he ran from the center of the camp.

Arrows flew at the soldiers. One lodged itself in a man's neck, while the other glanced off another soldier's armor. Before Sannoa knew what had happened, a giant net fell from the canopy above them, entangling most of the soldiers under it. She hacked at the hemp bindings Furiously.

"I'm sorry for your loss. Please, accept our gift as a truce. Between you and me, though, this was never about the clerics. I wish things could have been different," he said as his voice faded away.

"Come back here you coward!" she screamed.

Roaric hiked up the path to the camp. Dall sat on a tree stump at the center of camp, a bundle of armor at his feet. He looked up at Roaric as he approached, giving him a curt nod as he did.

"What's this?" Roaric asked, taking a seat across from the older man.

"Knight armor. Found it a few yards away, hidden in the trees over there," Dall said, jutting a bearded chin in the direction.

"Knight armor?" Roaric repeated, his eyebrows raised in surprise.

Dall nodded.

"Shit. Then it's a safe bet they know where we are."

"Most assuredly."

"Quil back?"

"Arrived just before you did," Dall replied.

"Assemble everyone then. I suspect we'll have company soon," Roaric said with a sigh, and stood. "I knew this would eventually come to an end. We likely don't have enough time to get everyone out of here, though, without some kind of delay or distraction."

"I'll assemble everyone while you come up with a plan to get us all out of here. What about the armor?" Dall asked.

"Leave it, we don't need it and it'll only bring trouble to anyone who tries to sell it."

Dall nodded in agreement.

"Have some men quickly tie our nets together and suspend it above the camp. We'll use that to trap the soldiers while everyone escapes," Roaric said.

"Aye," the older man said, extending a hand out to him. "It's been a pleasure serving with you."

"And you old friend," Roaric said, shaking it firmly. "Thank you for all you did."

"What will you do now?" Dall asked.

"I suspect the knight and her ilk won't let sleeping dogs lie. So I'll keep them looking at me. You and Quil, Manso should be able to live a normal life, should you choose to," Roaric said with a smile.

"Thank you," Dall said.

"It's the least I could do."

Dall pursed his lips in thought, then nodded again before making his way to the nearest tent to rouse those sleeping inside. Roaric watched a moment as he thought how lucky they were. If the armor hadn't been found, everyone in the camp would be either dead or arrested before supper. *The gods are on our side*, he thought to himself.

Chapter 9

FULL CIRCLE

ROARIC HEARD THE DOOR of the tavern open and close. He made no move to look over his shoulder to see who had entered. Instead, he downed the rest of his ale. The Cross Roads Tavern was quiet. There was only a handful of patrons, stemming from the fact it was late morning. Those that had stayed overnight had moved on. This emptiness gave it a serene, homey feel. The usual ruckus of merchants and caravan guards was nonexistent, leaving the crackling fireplace the only source of sound.

The smell of freshly baked bread, in preparation for the evening rush, engulfed the common room, adding to the welcoming feeling.

He felt the tip of a sword press against his back, causing him to freeze. After a second, however, he snorted and lifted a hand toward the barkeep. "Another round, please. Do you want anything? My treat."

"No," Sannoa said in a suppressed tone.

"Well, don't mind if I have one then?"

"You'll die all the same."

He nodded. "I'm sure."

The barkeep set the refilled mug down in front of Roaric and quickly moved away. Silence stretched between them as he slowly sipped his drink.

"Please, you're making me anxious. You sure you won't join me? I promise I won't run. You've won. You caught me," Roaric said.

Sannoa hesitated a moment then sheathed her sword. The barstool screamed along the wooden floor in a high-pitched screech. Its legs vibrated in protest as she moved it deliberately into place.

"Barkeep, please, get this knight a drink, on my tab," Roaric said, then whispered so only she could hear, "Not like I'll ever be able to pay it."

She protested, but it was too late. The barkeep sat a mug down in front of her.

"Please, join me. I mean, join me for a drink," Roaric said.

She stared at the mug a moment, then picked it up and drank deeply.

"You know it was never anything personal, right?"

"You assaulted followers of Gate'har. I take that personally."

"Fair, I suppose," Roaric said, and turned to face her. He had a chance to look at her. She was beautiful. Strong. Her hair was cut short, allowing him to see her face clearly as it held a permanent growl of disdain for him. He smiled at her then turned back to his mug. "So, are you here to drag me back to Xonthian City to stand trial, or just put me down here?"

"I haven't decided," she replied.

"I see."

The tension between them became palatable. Roaric took another drink from his mug and glanced sidelong at her. "You hungry?"

"Excuse me?"

"You eat, don't you?"

"Yes."

"If you're going to kill me, or hang me, I'd like to have one final meal that's not rotten jail food or earthworms," he said with a smile.

She stared at him blankly, unsure how to respond.

Taking it as a sign to continue, Roaric turned to the barkeep and raised a hand to beckon him over again. The older, plump man stepped closer and nodded a greeting.

"What can I get for you two?" he asked.

"Can we get some of that fresh bread? And whatever you have for lunch, or can make for lunch. For both of us please," Roaric said, untying his silver pouch from his belt. He dropped the entire thing on the counter. "This should more than cover whatever we order, right?"

"Oh yes, sir, most assuredly," the man said, picking it up and giving an appraising gaze before slipping it under the counter. "I shall return shortly."

"Thank you," Roaric said, turning back to look at Sannoa. He smiled to see she was still unsure how to respond. "You never did tell me your name. I'd like to know my captor at least."

She paused a moment as she contemplated his question. A finger dug at the hardwood counter as if trying to escape. "Sannoa," she said finally.

"Sannoa," Roaric said with a warm smile. "That is a unique name; beautiful too."

"Stop it," she replied.

"I'm sorry? Stop what?"

"You can't charm your way out of this. So stop trying," she growled.

"I assure you; I'm not going anywhere. I am not trying to charm you out of taking me in. As I said, you've caught me. I'll leave as soon as we're done with our meal. Deal?"

She only gave a curt nod in response.

"Why are you so angry with me? I killed a few acolytes; you killed a few mages and rebels. Are we not even?" he asked, glancing sidelong at her.

"No. You are a criminal, murdering my people as you go. You are harboring fugitives from the crown and the Goddess," she replied.

"Criminal, fine, yes. Harboring fugitives though? And harboring them against the crown and Goddess? I don't know about that. The way I see it, the crown didn't want those people pointing out the hypocrisy within their own government. Not like there is much difference between clerics and mages. Or how kingdoms use enchanted items. Is there? The crown had to ship them off somewhere. I simply gave them an alternative, giving them a chance to live outside the king's grasp. He didn't want them, so I gave them a home, a chance. And the Goddess? I seriously doubt she would exile her children to a godforsaken island like the Fire Isles. Would she? Would you? Honestly?"

"I-" she began, but closed her mouth again. Confusion flashed across her blue eyes. "You went against the king's decree."

"Since when do the clerics of Gate'har bow to the king? To any king?"

Once again there was no response. Sannoa glanced sidelong at the door, then back to him.

"Your men waiting outside? Did you really bring that many here to capture me?" he said with a laugh. "You overestimate my abilities and skills in combat. I've gotten lucky so far. And now, after months of running, it's left me tired."

"Is that why we're sitting here?" she asked.

"Yes. I'm done running. There is no point in it anymore," he said with a smile that didn't quite reach his eyes. A note of melancholy laced his voice.

"What makes you think I won't go after the rest of you rabble?" she asked.

"Do you even know who they are?"

She pursed her lips and took a swig from her mug.

"Good. Let's keep this between us. We had a good make of it, this game of cat and mouse. I'm tired though," he said with a heavy sigh. "Besides, I've heard that the mages are no longer interested in fighting against the exile. Some are even starting to go voluntarily. THAT... That should scare anyone."

"Oh? Why is that?"

The barkeep returned and sat down a plate of food for each of them, followed by a fork. A proud smile spread across his face. "Please, enjoy!"

"Thank you, kind sir," Roaric said, taking the fork. He dug in. "Oh man, this IS good, thank you."

The barkeep nodded continuously as he moved away to attend to another patron. A grin was plastered on the man's face.

"Why should the mage's actions scare us?" she repeated.

Roaric chewed his food hastily, then responded. "Because it means they are all amassing in one place. The power of so many disgruntled mages, on one island, ruled by fire? That's a powder keg sitting next to an open flame. Just waiting to explode."

Sannoa stared at him a moment then turned to the food in front of her. The two ate silently. When their plates were empty, the barkeep returned and took the empty tableware away, leaving the two soldiers to stare at their nearly empty mugs of ale.

"Well, I guess it's almost time. In another time, another place... I mean, I wish I had gotten to know you better outside of this discord we have going. I mean that, in the most sincere way possible," Roaric said, downing the rest of his ale. "Before we leave, can I ask you a question?"

She peered at him over the rim of her mug but said nothing.

"You didn't answer me, why are you angry with me?"

"Are you daft?" she growled.

"Well, yes, I suppose I am. But still, all things considered, can you give me an objective, honest answer? Is the oppression of the mage's freedom not an insult to you? To Gate'har?"

"You're a criminal," she replied with contempt.

"To whom? The crown doesn't know or care, do they? Has the Xonthian City Guard put a wanted poster out for me? Hells, do they even know what I've been doing down here? Or care? For the most part, we've gone unnoticed. A few mercenary guards or acolytes go missing, the crown doesn't care. The missing mages sure as hells don't warrant their ire. The king doesn't even want them anymore. After decades, no, millennia of service, he's tossing them out like some used parchment. Obviously, the mages are smart enough to never return. So, there is no need to draw questions or a glance down here from the kingdom. Gate'har clerics though, sure, I could see how the Angelic Island priests might be getting irritated with me killing their brothers and sisters. Is that why you're mad at me? Did I kill someone you knew? If so, please know I am sorry. Truly."

"Your wonton disrespect for life is what has drawn my rage," she replied.

"Rage? Rage is a strong word," he said, tapping his fingers thoughtfully on his empty mug. "Fine, fair enough. If I was only killing Mercs or city guards, would that have been better?"

"What? No! Of course not. You can't just go around killing people," she said, her eyes furrowed in confusion.

"Oh, yes, yes, of course. I meant that rhetorically speaking. Look, my point is, we didn't kill because we wanted to. We had to, to survive. We tried to free those mages with very few casualties. They are dead nonetheless. And I wish it weren't so. Do you know I still see their faces when I sleep? It's not you chasing me that has tired me out. It is their ghosts that I see, that has weighed on me."

"And that makes it all right? I should forgive you?"

He shrugged and turned around on the barstool, clapping his hands on his knees. "Well, I guess not. Not you, personally. I really am sorry I angered you. However, to your point, I was hoping you'd see things differently. Being as you're a woman of the Goddess. The Goddess of life, love, and forgiveness. Me? I have to live with the guilt of those deaths. I took men's and women's lives in pursuit of what I thought was just. No mage should have been tossed into the kiln of the Fire Isles, forgotten and alone. So, no, I should hang. I can't be forgiven. In the end, I don't want that weight."

He watched her as she stood. Her eyes never left his, as if she thought he would dash for the door. But he made no attempt to. He simply stood and walked toward the door, knowing the end was on the other side. He felt weightless for the first time in months. The burden he brought upon himself would come to an end soon.

Chapter 10

ONE QUESTION

Sannoa followed Roaric outside. It was warm, the sun high above them concealing the normally cool afternoons of mid-spring. The men she had left outside were half-encircled around the Cross Roads Tavern, spears and shields held at the ready as if expecting someone to bolt out the door. Before entering the establishment, she had hoped Roaric would have done just that. Saved her the hassle. Now, however, she wasn't so sure. As she approached the men with Roaric, her hand rested on the hilt of her sword, her eyes fixed on the back of the man's head.

She turned her attention to the men behind Roaric. "You men are dismissed. Thank you for your support. I can take it from here." She tossed a small pouch of silver at the closest man. "Enjoy a round of ale on me before you head home."

The soldiers peered around at one another then dispersed into the tavern, leaving Roaric and Sannoa standing in the road.

"Well, you really were expecting me to run," he said with a chuckle.

"Yes," she replied.

He held his wrists out to her. "Shall we go then?"

She looked at them, then into his grey eyes. They held no deception, no guile. They only looked tired, sunken in dark, baggy sockets. "Can I ask you a question?" she asked.

"Of course," Roaric replied.

"Why did you do it? Why did you risk your life for a bunch of mages you've never met? If you're not one, then why? Sure, the injustice of it. But that doesn't spur anyone into risking their life, does it? Not as much as you did. So why did you do it?"

"Ah... That question," he replied, dropping his outstretched hands heavily to his sides, "that is not easy to explain."

"Try."

"You're right, it wasn't only for the injustice. Do you ever go into battle, get that rush of adrenaline, the threat of death so close? It's sort of like that," he said, but then held his hands out and quickly added, "Not in a 'killing is thrilling' sort of way, no, no. Sorry, not what I meant. It was the rush to me, getting close to death, nearly being killed. It was the draw of the inverse of that that brought me back each time. I needed to feel nearly dying in order to feel. Maybe I should explain it this way—I enjoy life. All of it. To the fullest extent I can. I love often and with as much passion as my partners can handle. I eat and drink until my belly nearly bursts. I fight and survive tirelessly, so I can live. It's the rush, the life that rushes into the void of nearly dying that kept me going. I'm not doing a good job of explaining this without sounding like a creep."

"I... I actually understand," she said softly.

"You do?" he said, raising an eyebrow.

Sannoa sighed and shook her head as if trying to dislodge something. "When I was younger, my brother and I would go to the ocean, the reef southwest of our home. It's perfect for riding the waves there. We'd take these boards and ride them on our bellies, through the waves that'd crash against the shore. The adrenalin was nice, but it was the feeling of living that rushed through us after that made us keep going back."

Roaric only nodded in response.

"Still, it's no excuse for killing," she said.

"No, it's not. As I said, though, that is where you come in. You, or the Goddess, are the only ones who can forgive me. Absolve me, if you will. I did what I thought was just and found it gave me that connection to life. Was it selfish? Sure. If I could have ridden those waves with you, I probably would have done that instead. But here we are. Would I save those mages again? Yes. Yes, I would. Because I was doing good. I was offering freedom to the oppressed, the forsaken. When I meet the Goddess at the end of the gallows, I know my spirit will be pure. I lived justly. I have no regrets, no guilt."

Sannoa studied him a moment. She wanted to hate the man in front of her. It had been so easy for her to hate him. It drove her, kept her going. Now, however, she was finding it harder to kindle that flame of rage. He spoke true; there was no deception in his words. He wasn't fighting his judgment. He knew what waited for him in Xonthian City.

"You're not running?" she asked.

"I told you, I'm done," Roaric replied.

"You'll stand trial on Angelic Island, instead of Xonthian City," she said.

"Fine."

Sannoa sighed and motioned for him to follow as she began hiking down the hard-packed road headed east. She had no idea what was going on in her head.

Chapter 11

TRUCE

HE TREK FROM THE Cross Roads to Port Orlynns was long and rough on his feet, despite being able to get horses once they arrived in Roc Pass. His entire body ached in new places, and it was beginning to take its toll. He often considered running for safety, unwilling to continue the journey. But each time he thought about it, he turned his attention to the knight who followed close by. And each time he glanced at her, he felt something inside telling him to stay.

So, he swallowed the pain like dry, stale bread, and they continued. After several weeks of travel, they finally arrived in Port Orlynns. The city was a sprawling wood and stone settlement on the coast of Crescent Bay. The scent of the ocean, once a rare experience for him, had now become familiar again. It was just as potent, filled with the sharp tang of salt and the odor of decaying fish.

Tall pine trees embraced the city with green and red-brown arms that gave the entire place a frontier-like quality. While the forests around South Kelsa was full of lurking vines, shrubs, and moss, this was woodier and more earthen; pine needles blanketed the ground instead of decaying leaves.

Once again, he found himself in a tavern. The Broken Wheel had the best qualities of every other tavern he had visited. Smoky, grimy, filled with smells he would rather not know the source of, and ale that was passable at best. He glanced up at Sannoa, who was staring at him, a blank expression on her face.

"I think we're beyond me running away at this point, are we not?" he asked.

"Sorry, it's not that," she said, shaking her head and looking away. "You just puzzle me is all. I was so ready to skin you alive, and here you are, a man of your word, letting me drag you to your literal death, halfway across Xonthian."

"Not used to honesty, or is it something else?"

She lifted the mug to her lips and looked inside, then drank heavily from it. "I'm not used to men being anything but ignorant of what women want."

Roaric arched a brow. "Clearly you haven't been with me long enough. I know nothing of what women want. Least of all you."

She chuckled.

"Still, after weeks of traveling with you, I can safely say I don't know you, and wouldn't presume to. It's not my place. Further, right now, you hold my life in your Goddess-faring hands. Why in her name would I displease you?"

She laughed out loud this time. "Still trying to charm your way out of this?"

"Well, no, but if I were, is it working?"

"No," she said with a smile.

"Let me ask you a serious question, if I may?"

"Of course."

"When we were at the Cross Roads, why didn't you disarm me? I still carry my sword. You've made no attempt to confiscate the weapon this entire time. I don't know you, that's true. Likewise could be said of me, you don't know me. I could have slit your throat a million times before tonight," Roaric said, watching her closely for a reaction.

Sannoa's face returned to a blank mask of indifference. Her blue eyes flickered back and forth as if she was trying to figure out an escape. In the end, she shrugged and sat back. "If we're being honest?"

"Please."

"I didn't even think about it," she stated matter-of-factly.

It was Roaric s turn for laughter. "All that rage and you forgot I'm the enemy?"

"Are you?"

This caught Roaric by surprise; his laughter caught in his throat and forced him to cough the lump out that formed there. "You sure made that clear; I'm to be held accountable to the clerics before the Goddess Gate'har. Does that not make you my enemy?"

"If we're being honest with one another, I guess technically it does. I told you I hated you; I was full of rage. But it wasn't you I was mad at. I was mad... Well, I was mad at you, but I was also mad at the luck I had. I worked hard for the position of guarding mages to their exile. As a knight of Gate'har, I had to work twice as hard for the honor of being a guard. My first charge as a knight, outside the walls of Gate'har Citadel. And you ruined it. I was mad at you, sure, yes. But not because of you. You hadn't personally offended me, but because of the situation you placed me in," she said with a furrowed brow.

"If it means anything to you, I'm sorry. Truly. I suppose it really never occurred to me how our actions would affect others. Beyond those that were killed, of course. I figured, or rather told myself, those casualties were just as likely to come from bandits. So, I justified those we killed as nothing more than that. And for that, I am also sorry."

"Guess it doesn't matter now, does it?" she asked.

"As I said, I would do it again. But no, it doesn't matter. And I never meant anything personally against you," he said, taking a swig from his mug.

"Should I take your sword away?" she asked finally.

He chuckled. "I would not draw it against you, but if you have to take it, then I shall surrender it willingly."

Someone bumped into him, causing him to splash the remainder of his mug across the table and onto Sannoa's lap. He stood and turned to face the person who had assaulted him, only to be met with a right hook. Chaos exploded in the tavern as shouts and slurs flew through the air. Roaric and Sannoa barely managed to slide out from the melee and into the streets, leaving behind not only the rest of their meal but a warm place to sleep. He sighed and turned his attention to her; she was trying feebly to wipe the drink off her armor and trousers.

She looked up at him, and the two started laughing.

Chapter 12

<hr>

DEATH HAS A NAME

T HE TWO WALKED TOWARD the docks on the east side of the city. The Temple of Gate'har was a compound, where several large sailing vessels were docked inside a walled-off section. Roaric and Sannoa sat down on a crate that faced the docks several yards away. It was too early in the evening to gain access to the compound where their ship awaited them. The plan had been to stay the night in the Broken Wheel. Now that chaos had overtaken the place, neither of them felt like returning.

The moon was bright above them, its silver light sparkling on the gently flowing tide that rolled in from the ocean beyond the protective embrace of the Crescent Bay. The smell, although more pungent here than it had been in the city, was more tolerable. Possibly because Roaric had grown more accustomed to its lingering presence.

There were very few people mulling around the pier. It was well past time for most of the workers to be home, asleep, while city guards were likely busy at the Broken Wheel. Roaric sighed and looked out over the bay.

"Well, I have to say, this is a sight. You lived near the ocean?" he asked, suddenly remembering the story about her brother.

"I lived in Yenzu," she said, looking out over the water as if remembering something.

"Yenzu, wow, I never met anyone from there," he said with a smile.

"For being a resort town, you sure don't see many of us outside of it. Most that live there work there, so there's no need to venture beyond the deserts."

"Why did you?"

She sighed. "My brother, the one I mentioned, died on one of our trips to the beach. The waves were giant and rough. We shouldn't have gone. But they were like nothing we had seen before, perfect tubes to ride our boards through. One of them crashed sooner than he expected, and he went under. He got caught on a reef. Nearly gutted him. I was barely able to get him to shore. Before I could, though, he had lost too much blood. He died in my arms."

"I-I don't know what to say. Sorry doesn't seem adequate," he said, pausing slightly to look at her.

"It's ok, I appreciate the sentiment."

"Is that why you call yourself death? As penance for his?"

"What?" she said with a shocked look on her face.

"When we first met, you said your name was death. Is that your nickname? Because you blame yourself for his?"

"Oh," she said, glancing back at the water. She sat a moment before nodding and saying, "I guess maybe it is."

"Can I say how much bullshit that is?"

"What? Why?"

"Did you cause his injuries? Did you make him ride that wave, knowing it might be dangerous?"

"No, I guess not."

"Then don't blame yourself. That's bullshit," he said with a grin.

She sighed heavily and sat back against the crate.

"Don't ever blame yourself for the actions of others. I did what I did. That's why I gave all those that followed me a chance to escape. I made my decision long ago to help those mages. Along the way, others joined me, sure, but I didn't make them. And when it came time to part ways, I again gave them the choice. I don't blame them for wanting to leave and not face the judgment of the Goddess, no more than you should be blaming yourself for your brother's choice to enjoy life and risk it for the glory of riding one hell of a wave," he said with a slight chuckle. "Gods, I bet that would be fun."

"It was," she said, a smile in her voice.

The sound of wood creaking snapped their attention toward the pier. A half dozen men walked toward them. Sannoa shot Roaric a glance, and he shrugged in response to her silent question. He didn't know who they were.

The two stood and faced the approaching men. They wore torn, grungy clothing, as if beasts had frayed the ends with gnashing teeth. The smell of ale wafted from their breath, a stench noticeable even at the arm's length away they were.

"Can we help you?" Sannoa asked.

"Aye, darlin', you can. You an your boy there owe us sittin' fees," the man in front said, holding a rusty sword out toward them.

"No, we don't. So get lost," Sannoa said with a growl.

"Look at this, boys, this cleric thinks she can take us all on," the man said with a hollow laugh.

Sannoa glanced at Roaric, who unsheathed his weapon. He knew this wouldn't end without a fight. He nodded at her, and she did the same. The two attacked in unison.

Roaric had two bandits simultaneously attacking him. He dodged the first stab toward him, then parried the second. He kept them busy while Sannoa dealt with three others. There were two men beyond, waiting for an opening to join. There was, however, only so much room on the dock.

The bandit tried to slash Roaric's midsection, but Roaric was able to skip the blade aside and respond with a punch to the man's face. The man stumbled, and before Roaric could press the assault, the second man renewed his attack.

Roaric twisted out of the way and came down with his blade on the man's back, fileting it open. The man howled in pain and stumbled forward.

The other man thrust his sword at Roaric; again he managed to parry the blade aside and punch him. This caused the bandit to swear angrily in response. Roaric followed up the punch with a front kick, sending the man flying off the edge of the dock.

Sannoa pulled her sword from the gut of a bandit moments before the others attacked her. Roaric lunged at them and deflected several of their blows. With a quick flick of his wrist, he managed to dispatch two more, while Sannoa fended off the remainder. In the confusion, Roaric lost sight of their leader, who had worked his way behind Sannoa.

He suddenly noticed the man had gone missing in the scuffle. He glanced over his shoulder and saw the leader lunge toward Sannoa from the corner of his vision.

"Look ou—" Roaric said, jumping in front of the attack. There was no pain; all he felt was the man's wet breath on his cheek. The stench of beer overwhelmed him.

He pushed away instinctively and saw the man's head fall from his neck, splashing into the water below. With an offhand, detached sense of what was going on, he glanced down and saw blood stream from the stab wound. He suddenly felt pain, as if acknowledging it had materialized the feeling. He turned to see Sannoa fighting the last handful of men. He took a step and felt lightning shoot up his side and back. He stumbled forward, causing the tip of his blade bury itself in the wood plank of the dock.

Roaric grit his teeth and glanced up. The last bandit fell at her feet. He smiled and fell forward. He suddenly felt sleepy. The smell of saltwater was soothing, and the sound of the gently rolling waves crashing against the rocks of the pier wall washed away the fear he felt creeping up from the depths of his belly.

Gentle hands lifted his head, and he opened his eyes to see Sannoa glancing down at him.

"Hold on, I think I can heal you," she said. She whispered a prayer to the Goddess and set her hand on his wound.

He smiled up at her. "It's ok."

"No, no it's not, damnit! You will hang for your crimes! You don't get to die like this!" she said.

He tried laughing, then coughed up blood. "Die like what? A dog in a common street brawl?"

"No, damnit! You know what I mean," she said.

"Tell me," he said.

"For saving my life! Just, just don't die!"

His smile slid slightly, and every muscle in his body felt heavy.

She cursed herself. "Goddess, please. Not again."

"I... I don't blame you," he whispered softly. "Live in peace, Sannoa."

She looked down at him, her jaw clenched tightly in anger. "You... I forgive you. I absolve you, Roaric. I... I'm sorry."

He tried to raise a hand up to her, and she took it as his last breath escaped his lips in a slow, steady whisp. His vision pinholed around her face, drowning the edges of world in darkness. His last memory was of his own childhood. And the dog he lost. He wondered if he would get to see him again.

Sannoa held Roaric's head in her lap and rocked gently back and forth. The nightmare of her brother's death repeated in her mind over and over again. She looked up at the large, silver moon and yelled at it. As if Gate'har could hear her.

Dawn approached several hours later, and still she sat there, cradling the dead man's head in her lap. She didn't know him, didn't owe him anything. She couldn't figure out why she was still there with him. She told herself every lie she could come up with, but nothing felt real. Deep down she knew why. Deep down, she knew the reason she was still there was he had shown her the truth, the reason she had joined Gate'har in the first place. It wasn't to serve blind justice. It wasn't because she knew how to heal wounds. It wasn't to play caravan guard. It was to serve the Goddess of Life. It was to ensure that those who didn't deserve death were not alone during their final breath. She was a shepherd to them. She was death.

Acknowledgments

First and foremost, I want to thank you the reader for taking the time to read this anthology. I want to thank D.W. for putting up with me, and for taking a chance on these stories. For pushing for the very best stories, and for the time that's involved in publishing them.

I want to thank my wife for all her help as always. The road will be long and hard going forward, much like any growth. We'll do it together though and forge a path out of the fire's that burn around us! To dark?

I want to thank everyone who's helped me become a better writer, there are far too many to name and I'd be afraid I missed someone. So thank you.

There is much more to come. So please, follow all my social media and keep up to date with future content. I wouldn't be here without you, so again, thank you.

-Daniel

Social Media Links: tigerforce.net/links.html

About the author

Daniel Dickinsons' writing first appeared in an annual publication with his short story "Escape from Ogre Island." He has self-published two other stories, "Gathering Tide" and the newly released "Aggression Factor." He is a frequent contributor to the Arizona Author Association's quarterly newsletter.

At the age of ten, he began creating a realistic realm, Xonthian, in which his characters come to life, allowing the reader to become a part of that diverse world. Xonthian continues to evolve. The heroes, Tiger and Bree, begin their sagas alone until circumstances bring them together. Future projects include a weird wild west tale, set in the world of Xonthian, and a novel featuring the titular heroes Tiger and Bree.

Daniel is a proud father with a beautiful wife. He enjoys traveling and photography, as well as food and art. One of his many hobbies is taking his daughter and grandkids camping at least twice a year.

Camp Slasher Lake: Volume One, winner of the 2023 Spatterpunk Award for Best Anthology.

A tribute to the glorious slasher movies of the 1980s, Volume 1.

Featuring stories from: John Adam Gosham, Gerri R. Gray, Patrick C. Harrison III, Carlton Herzog, D.W. Hitz, Derek Austin Johnson, J.D. Kellner, Brian McNatt, Nicholas Stella, & Vincent Wolfram

Available now from online bookstores or Fedowar.com.

Gods are Born by D.W. Hitz

This is not the world you know. When aliens crashed on Earth, everything changed. Humanity has been decimated by predators and plague. Electromagnetic waves render most technology useless. The survivors are afflicted by strange mutations—some troubling, others amazing.

Gods are Born is a mature sci-fi read with elements of horror and graphic violence that follows the paths of seven extraordinary beings as they struggle to survive, find peace within themselves, and ultimately, defeat the King and something far worse than they can imagine.

Available now from online bookstores or Fedowar.com.

Thank you for reading.